th**e**ashleys

more books by
melissa de la cruz

The Au Pairs

The Au Pairs: Skinny-dipping

The Au Pairs: Sun-kissed

The Au Pairs: Crazy Hot

Angels on Sunset Boulevard

Blue Bloods

Masquerade: A Blue Bloods Novel

Fresh Off the Boat

Cat's Meow

How to Become Famous in Two Weeks or Less

The Fashionista Files:
Adventures in Four-Inch Heels and Faux Pas

Girls Who Like Boys Who Like Boys

melissa de la cruz

thashleys

mix

aladdin mix

NEW YORK   LONDON   TORONTO   SYDNEY

ALADDIN MIX

Simon & Schuster Children's Publishing Division

1230 Avenue of the Americas, New York, NY 10020

Copyright © 2008 by Melissa de la Cruz

All rights reserved, including the right of reproduction in whole or in part in any form.

ALADDIN PAPERBACKS and related logo are registered trademarks of Simon & Schuster, Inc.

Aladdin Mix is a trademark of Simon & Schuster, Inc.

Designed by Karin Paprocki

The text of this book was set in Mrs. Eaves.

Manufactured in the United States of America

First Aladdin Mix edition January 2008

2 4 6 8 10 9 7 5 3 1

Library of Congress Control Number 2007937055

ISBN-13: 978-1-4169-3406-6

ISBN-10: 1-4169-3406-5

For Mattea Katharine Johnston, my sweet baby girl
and
Jennie Kim, BFF, for spilling the beans, sharing her
memories, and always being an inspiration

You wanted to be a member of the most powerful
clique in school. If I wasn't already the head of it,
I'd want the same thing.
—**Heather Chandler,** *Heathers*

I refuse to join any club
that would have me as a member.
—**Groucho Marx**

the ashleys

1

THE NOT-SO-NEW GIRL

LAUREN PAGE SMOOTHED DOWN THE FOLDS OF her short plaid skirt and crossed her legs so that she could admire the shiny new black-and-white Chanel spectator oxfords on her feet a little better. They looked so cute with her thick cashmere socks scrunched down just above the ankle, she thought. She'd been wearing the same green plaid uniform to Miss Gamble's all her life, but she was in the upper form now—seventh grade—which meant saying good-bye to her boring old Buster Browns and hello to the first boy-girl dance with the hotties from Gregory Hall, which was only three weeks away. And as far as she was concerned, upper form meant a whole new Lauren.

She leaned back on the plush, baby-soft leather seat in her dad's sparkling new Bentley Continental and pressed a button that flipped a mirror on the console in front of her.

Sometimes she couldn't believe it herself. The girl who

smiled back from the mirror looked nothing like the old Lauren. This one had pin-straight chestnut brown hair that fell softly on her shoulders and shone with reddish and caramel gold highlights, a killer Mystic spray tan, and cheekbones so sharp they could cut ice. Lauren felt a little like those young starlets who lost so much weight and started looking so hot that people whispered they'd had major plastic surgery. Lauren turned her head sideways to try and get a good look at her profile. Her nose certainly looked different now that her baby fat had melted away.

"Nervous?" a voice asked from the driver's seat.

Lauren stopped preening and raised a carefully plucked-by-Anastasia eyebrow at the speaker via the rearview mirror. "Should I be?" she asked Dex, her father's seventeen-year-old intern and personal pet project who, when he wasn't dreaming up online schemes for her father as part of his "regular" job, was part brother, part bodyguard, and full-time chauffeur.

"Maybe, because you're still ugly." Dex laughed.

"Takes one to know one," Lauren said, sticking her tongue out at him and feeling suddenly anxious. What if Dex was right? She checked the mirror again. A smoldering, gray-eyed brunette beauty glared back at her. No, there was no way. He was just being a smart-ass as usual.

"You shouldn't care so much what people think. Seriously,

it's not attractive," he said, as he took a sharp turn down a curve and Lauren had to clutch at the hand rest to keep from sliding down the length of the backseat.

"Um, did Dr. Phil die or something? Because 'Dr. Dex' has a slightly stupid ring to it," Lauren retorted. *Easy for him to say*, she thought. Dex had always been popular and was criminally good-looking, even after he shaved off his pretty-boy curls to sport a Justin Timberlake buzz cut. He was smart, too—graduating early from prep school, where he had been captain of the lacrosse, crew, and soccer teams, and taking the year off before enrolling in Stanford's accelerated computer program. Whereas Lauren had been going to Miss Gamble's all her life, and no one ever talked to her unless it was to ask for answers to the social studies quiz.

But all that was going to change this year.

She looked out the dark-tinted car window at the familiar roller-coaster streets of San Francisco's Pacific Heights. The exclusive neighborhood's palatial Victorian mansions didn't look intimidating anymore; some of them looked small, even downright dinky.

Life had taken a turn for the ultra-luxe ever since YourTV.com went public last year. The video-sharing website was her father's brainchild, a deceptively simple idea that allowed anyone on the planet to be a star in the cyberuniverse. The site exploded suddenly and without warning, catapulting the family from their shoebox-size Mission District one-bedroom walk-up to a grand estate of their own in the Marina, with an unparalleled view of the bay and their own helipad on the roof.

Dad was the newly crowned king of Silicon Valley and had made the covers of *Fortune* and *Forbes*, and Mom had gone from protesting animal testing on the sidewalk to chairing benefit dinners for African orphans. And Lauren, who had made do with thrift-store castoffs and clearance-bin remnants all her life, suddenly found herself at designer boutiques on Maiden Lane with a personal shopper hanging on her every word.

Last year she was a financial-aid pity case, fretting over whether anyone at school would notice that her blue cashmere sweater had been bought secondhand at the school's charity shop. This year her sweater was a nine-hundred-dollar one with a fancy Italian label. Lauren had been worried about getting a stain on it, until her dad—who used to pay the grocery bill with change from the kitchen jar whenever his graduate teaching assistant stipend ran out—had told her that she wouldn't have to worry about anything ever again. At least not where pricey designer clothes were concerned. Well, then. Bring on the twelve-ply Mongolian cashmere.

Lauren grabbed a tall, frosty Voss water bottle from the

4

mini-fridge hidden in the side compartment to calm her nerves.

Because Dex was right. She was a little nervous. A head-to-toe Emma Roberts—like makeover was one thing, but there were still the Ashleys to contend with. Lauren could see them now, giving her the daily head-to-toe fashion evaluation and shaking their heads in mock disgust. Even if there was a school uniform and all students were supposed to look the same to eliminate "status consciousness," the Ashleys always looked like they stepped out of a J. Crew catalog, while Lauren looked like she'd stumbled out of an old *Full House* episode. They never let her forget it either.

Lauren clenched her jaw. What if they saw through her six-hundred-dollar haircut and carefully accessorized uniform and decided she was just the same old dork she had always been?

The old Lauren was a meek, frizzy-haired girl who sat in the back, whom no one ever paid attention to until her name was called at the end of every year during Prize Day, when the whole school gathered in the main hall, all the girls wearing ivy-covered garlands in their hair while the headmistress gave out the awards for the top student in every subject. She would stand for what seemed like an excruciatingly long time while Miss Burton read out the list of awards she'd received, in every subject except gym—mercifully, she escaped that one mortification.

What if they looked at her and saw the same Lauren from last year?

She would not allow that to happen. She dug her Black Satin manicure into the Bentley's thick upholstery, leaving ugly grooves in the Italian leather. Uh-oh. That was going to cost a fortune to fix. Then she remembered with relief that a fortune was exactly what she had right now. And like Angelina Jolie, she was going to use her money to do something *good* for a change.

First she was going to join the Ashleys. And then she was going to destroy them. She wanted to change the world one day, and she was going to start by making the seventh grade a better place to be.

The car pulled up to the main gates, where a slew of expensive European cars were lined up, depositing their precocious charges on the sidewalk—the rosy-cheeked daughters of the most elite families in the Bay Area. Several girls who lived down the street in the multimillion-dollar townhouses Lauren had just passed were casually walking up the hill, Marc by Marc Jacobs messenger bags slung across their chests.

Lauren spied the Ashleys in their usual before-school hangout by the stone bench in front of the playground, the three of them holding matching venti decaf soy lattes and

looking beyond bored. They looked so sweet and innocent—
not at all like the soul-destroying creatures they really were.
She inhaled and said a little prayer to whatever gods watched
over made-over twelve-year-olds with secret intentions.

Today was the first day of the rest of her new life.

2

ASHLEY SPENCER IS ONLY
ALLERGIC TO WEAKNESS

"AHEM. MISS ASHLEY, YOUR MOTHER WANTS to remind you to take your EpiPen."

"I will. God, she's such a nag!" Ashley Spencer thanked the elderly butler who had been in her mother's family for years and dismissed him from the kitchen with a nod. She rolled her eyes and stuffed the slim silver needle for injecting the shot of epinephrine—the only thing that would keep her alive in case she even *breathed* nut aroma—into her puffy Fendi Moncler Spy bag's secret compartment in the handle, next to her strawberry-scented lip gloss.

Her mom was *so* Nazi about her allergy, ever since she'd almost killed Ashley on her fourth birthday, when the exquisite French chocolate cake she served at the party turned out to have had a trace amount of hazelnuts in the batter.

Since then Ashley refrained from eating anything that

wasn't cooked for her by the Spencers' gourmet chef. Her nut-free lunch was already prepared in a cute Japanese lunchbox that she'd found in Tokyo that summer. It was made of cool white plastic and decorated with bug-eyed anime characters. Tokyo was *so* eye-opening—the style there was *très* unconventional, and Ashley had bought the lunchbox in an attempt to emulate the famous Harajuku Girls. But now, looking at it, she briefly wondered if the lunchbox was a little too goofy and "sixth grade" somehow and made a mental note to find out if there were such things as Chanel Thermos containers.

She turned off the mirrored flat-screen TV that hung in the breakfast nook and left her cereal bowl and juice glass on the island counter for the maid to clean. The clock on the smooth, stainless-steel face on the Thermador oven told her it was twenty-five minutes to the first bell, but instead of dashing out the door she took her time, removing a breath strip from a tiny plastic case in her pocket and letting the gooey green film melt on her tongue while she gathered her things. She was supposed to be at the Fillmore Starbucks by now, and the other Ashleys were probably waiting, but she didn't care. They could wait. As if they would walk to school without her, *hello*.

"How about a kiss?" asked her mother, coming out of her study and finding Ashley brushing her hair in front of the grand Louis Quinze mirror hanging in the main hall. "Did Darby remind you to pack your allergy kit?"

"For the hundredth time, yes, Mom. And careful with the hair," Ashley ordered, putting her hairbrush away and allowing herself to be kissed on both cheeks. She wrinkled her nose at her mother's heavy patchouli perfume. Couldn't Mom switch to something like Chanel No. 5? She gave her mother's outfit a cool once-over. "I hope you're not wearing that for this afternoon's tea," she commented, letting the inflection in her voice tell her mother that it wasn't a good idea.

Matilda Spencer crossed her arms and gave her daughter a bemused look. "I'm not, but why, is there something wrong with it?"

"Mom, 1998 called, they want their jeans back. Could you please put on the new skinny jeans we bought at Saks on Saturday?"

Ashley shook her head. Her mother was the most beautiful woman she knew, and not just because they looked so eerily alike they could be sisters. The two of them had long, lustrous golden hair; clear, cornflower blue eyes; and pale ivory skin without a hint of a freckle. If Mom was Gwyneth Paltrow, Ashley was just a younger, smoother version, both of them delicate blondes with enviably thin arms and speedy metabolisms.

Their similarities ended with fashion, though. Ashley was

always red-carpet-ready, even when she was just going to school, finding numerous ways to accessorize her uniform— wearing thick black tights instead of the chunky socks she'd made so popular with the plaid skirt last year, finding high-heeled patent-leather Mary Janes that fit the saddle-shoe requirement, and wearing James Perse T-shirts underneath the V-neck sweaters instead of the tidy blouses with their Peter Pan collars. Her mother, unfortunately, stuck to a casual wardrobe of Peruvian handmade knits, plastic Crocs, and jeans she'd owned since college at UC Berkeley. Matilda never really cared too much about clothes. It was *such* a waste.

Her mother was hosting the annual Miss Gamble's mother-daughter "welcome back" tea in the sunroom that afternoon with Lili's mom, and Ashley wouldn't normally care what anyone thought, since her mother was always the prettiest woman in the room, but sometimes she wished Matilda would make more of an effort to look more fashionable. Lili's mom was always totally done up in the latest designer duds, with perfect hair, nails, and makeup, and she looked like the quintessential private-school parent.

While Ashley chastised her mom for her fashion sense, she heard her father come jogging down the stairs in a holey T-shirt and yoga pants, his guru following behind.

"Off to school, precious?" he asked, doing sun salutations in the foyer while Bodhi helped balance him. "Ready for the new year? You know you'll kick ass! Won't she, my love?" he asked, turning to his wife and giving her a kiss on the nose.

Her mother giggled and looped her arm around her husband's, and for a frightening moment it looked like the two of them would actually start to make out in front of their daughter, but thankfully her father got distracted by his trainer, and the cringe-worthy display of affection was averted. Ashley breathed a sigh of relief.

When she was little, she loved having her parents at home all the time, but now it was getting annoying. Neither of them worked in any real sense—Dad "managed" the family trusts and Mom worked on her "art," both of them having inherited a huge chunk of change from their families. Which meant they had ample time to suffocate their only child, although they tried to be "cool" parents: Bedtime was flexible on the weekends, they didn't nag her about her grades too much, and her mom didn't nose around her online profiles like other mothers did.

"You're not going to be here for the tea, are you?" she asked her father. "Please don't." She didn't want him wandering around the house barefoot in his sweats, or strumming his guitar while the whole seventh-grade class tittered. Seriously, parents could be so embarrassing. The *Nob Hill Gazette* had once crowned her parents San Francisco's "It Couple," but that was a long time ago, before she was even born. They were such goofballs now, it was hard to imagine them as ever being so superglamorous.

Ashley allowed herself to be hugged by the two of them and walked out the door, checking once again to make sure she had that antiallergy shot in her purse. It made her feel better knowing it was there, especially since almost no one knew about her condition, and she liked to keep it that way.

No way in hell was she going to be dumped in with Cass Franklin, that freak who had to eat in her own screened-off quarantined section of the refectory, alienated from all the other kids. Ashley had pretended for so long that she liked living on nothing but yogurt and spelt bread and raw vegetables that she almost believed it.

She was Ashley Spencer, the undisputed, unshakable leader of the Ashleys. No one told her what she could and couldn't eat.

Owning up to her allergy was admitting weakness. Seventh grade was a saddle-shoe jungle. And Ashley Spencer made sure everyone marched to the beat of her own iPod.

3

BFF OR WORST ENEMY?
FOR ASHLEY LI,
IT'S THE SAME THING

OW MUCH LONGER DID SHE HAVE TO WAIT?
Another five minutes? Ten? Fifteen? Her
mother would go ballistic if she got slapped
with a late notice on the first day of school. Three late
notices and you had to face the Honor Board—which was
kind of out of the question for her, since she was *on* the
Honor Board.

Ashley Li checked the time on the dangling golden lock of
her tan leather Hermès Kelly watch, which she wore strapped
around her wrist like a lariat. If they weren't at Miss Gamble's
in fifteen minutes, Miss Moos, the dreaded school secretary
with the creepy hair weave and onion-bagel breath, would soon
be ringing their parents, inquiring in that quavery voice of
hers as to why their little girls weren't in school that morning.

She took a sip from her cardboard coffee cup. Chai soy decaf latte. It tasted like extra-hot crap, but she pretended to like it because Ashley Spencer loved it, and the point of being friends with Ashley Spencer—the whole point of being in the Ashleys—was that they all liked and did the same things. They had decided back in fourth grade that the Ashley thing was too confusing, so they would go by very cute nicknames instead. All except for Ashley Spencer, of course, who somehow retained the right to be called "Ashley." Lili was a much chicer name than Ashley anyway, Lili decided.

Where was the biatch? It drove her crazy how Ashley never seemed to notice the time.

You'd think the girl would at least *try* to be on time for the first day of junior high. Lili sighed. She'd have to lie to her mom again to explain the disciplinary note.

Whenever Lili messed up at school, she was sure to feel the wrath of (Nancy) Khan. Her mother, who had kept her maiden name and used to be the highest-paid female partner at Willbanks, Eliot, and Dumforth (and before that, editor at the *Harvard Law Review*), was now a full-time SAHM: a stay-at-home mom—or in her case, a socialite-at-home mom, serving on all of the committees and volunteer boards at Miss Gamble's. She didn't accept anything less than perfection from her only daughter.

She should just leave. Forget Ashley. Yeah, right. As if

she could ever desert her best friend. That was the problem. Ashley could make anything better, more fun, and less completely mundane. She thought about the stickers from last year that Ashley had made for them to put on select lockers. The stickers read "The Ashleys: SOA" in script on silver foil. No one but the three of them knew what the letters stood for, and it drove the whole class crazy trying to guess. SOA stood for "Seal of Approval," which should have been glaringly obvious, since only the cool girls in class got the sticker.

Lili gripped her coffee cup tightly, took an agonized sip of the drink, and contemplated tossing it into the trash. They'd gotten into trouble for the stickers once the faculty got wind of the incident; the girls were chastised because their little prank promoted "clique culture," which was supposedly against school policy. Uh-huh. Good luck with that.

Ashley supposedly had a surprise for them, and Lili had no choice but to wait or be left out of the fun. Her other best friend, Ashley Alioto, had found something better to do than wait around for Ashley. A. A. had arrived right on time, just as Lili had, but she'd disappeared once they'd gotten their lattes. Maybe she had decided to ditch Ashley, but most likely she was just on the phone to that "boyfriend"—air quotes definitely intended—of hers again.

Lili yawned and stretched on the wooden chair. She reached behind her to make sure her new Fendi Moncler Spy bag was still hanging there. The puffy tote was the same one that Ashley would be carrying and the same one that A. A. had carelessly plopped down on the seat across from hers. They had bought them together a few weeks ago. Lili had angled for the fire-engine red version, but Ashley had convinced her that beige was a more practical color for them. A. A., of course, had settled for the beige without complaint.

Lili noticed an old Chinese lady smiling at her from across the room. Old Chinese ladies were always smiling at her. She figured she probably reminded them of their granddaughters or something. They were always patting her on the head and saying, *"Piao liang, piao liang"* (pretty, pretty). Lili always smiled back. She knew how to take a compliment.

Her jet black hair fell just below her shoulders, and today she was wearing it in soft curls. She had fine, delicate features, slightly almond-shaped eyes, a tiny chin, and a flawless, caramel complexion. People always said she looked like Ziyi Zhang from those crazy martial arts movies, but maybe that was because there were no other Asian actresses to compare her to. She didn't think she looked a bit like Ziyi Zhang, but she liked hearing it anyway. Speaking of things she liked to hear . . .

"Hi, pretty!" called a clear, singsong voice from the entrance of the shop.

She turned. Ashley had finally arrived. Lili got up from her chair so fast she almost knocked over her coffee cup.

"Hi, pretty!" she gushed back. "Omigod!" she exclaimed, slapping her hands on her hips in dismay.

"What?"

"Your bag!" Lili accused, pointing to the offending accessory.

"I know! Don't you love?" Ashley grinned, holding it up to the light.

"It's *red!*" said Lili indignantly. "You said we were all getting beige!"

"I changed my mind," Ashley said, shrugging. *"I'm always red,"* she added, quoting from their favorite movie, *Heathers*.

"Ha-ha," Lili deadpanned sourly. "But now we don't match." She frowned. "We were all supposed to get the same one."

"You and A. A. still match," Ashley pointed out. "What's the big deal? It's just a bag, Lil. Chill out."

Lili pasted a smile on her face. It was just a bag. Ashley was right. She was Lili's best friend, and so what if she'd changed her mind? Lili could have changed her mind just as easily, but of course, the thought would never have occurred to her. They had an agreement. Now instead of three Ashleys, she and A. A. would look like backup singers to the main Ashley. This was so *Dreamgirls*. But if Ashley didn't watch out, Lili was going to Jennifer Hudson her one day.

"Is there time for me to get my chai?" Ashley said, angling up to the counter.

No, thought Lili.

"Uh-huh," she said instead. It wouldn't make a difference. Ashley collected late notices like Repetto ballerina flats.

"I'm totally parched. Where's A. A.?" asked Ashley, moving to the pickup section and looking around the busy Starbucks.

"Here." A tall, tanned girl strode toward them. She wore her hair in a pair of signature pigtails. Only a girl as gorgeous as Ashley Alioto could get away with such a juvenile hairstyle. A. A. towered over both of her friends. She was built like a tennis player—slim, toned, and tanned—and walked with an athlete's bouncy step.

"Hi, pretty!" Ashley cooed.

"Hi, pretty!" A. A. greeted back.

They kissed each other on both cheeks the way they'd seen fashion models do it on the Style Network.

"You got the red," A. A. noted, stroking the soft leather of Ashley's new bag. "I like."

Lili tried not to gag. It was so obvious what A. A. was doing: sucking up to Ashley as usual. It would be sickening if it wasn't so sincere. A. A. had the well-deserved reputation as being the nicest of the Ashleys; everyone in class called her mega-dece. More likely she was just too spacey to be mean. Lili tried to feel annoyed but decided it was too much trouble. And besides, frowning caused wrinkles at some point. Only ugly girls had reason to frown, and Lili's life was as perfect as any twelve-year-old could hope for.

"Is that a new lunchbox?" asked Lili, noticing Ashley's new Japanese case. "Where'd you get?"

"Tokyo," Ashley replied. "You don't think it's too sixth grade?" she asked.

Lili shook her head a little less than vigorously. "No way."

Ashley smiled, only slightly reassured, but continued, "Omigod. I totally forgot. I brought treats." She fished around in her Fendi bag and handed out what looked like three plastic toys. "Surprise! They're Prada Robot Charms. They only sell them in Tokyo. Accessories for your accessories. Don't you love?"

Lili and A. A. squealed in delight and immediately attached them to their bags like Ashley did.

"See?" Ashley said, picking up her cup. "Now we all match."

Lili nodded, appeased. No one else at school would have the robot charms.

"Ready?" asked Ashley.

The two others nodded, and with arms linked, the three of them walked out of the Starbucks and up the hill toward school.

4

A. A. IS JUST
ASHLEY ALIOTO'S NICKNAME,
NOT HER BRA SIZE

EEPING AN EYE ON HER TWO FRIENDS WHO were walking slightly in front of her, nearly identical handbags dangling from their elbows, Ashley Alioto tapped a message on her cell phone. TALK 2 U L8R TXT ME I HAVE RE<< I HAVE A BRK @ 11.

Silly. She'd almost texted him saying she had *recess* at eleven! She turned off her phone, rubbed the rhinestones embedded on its stainless silver cover, and exhaled. She'd caught herself just in the nick of time, thank God.

He was just *sooo* amazing. She was *totally* into him. And it was mutual, she could tell. Not that he'd said anything of the kind, but after all, they'd only just met a month ago online. Their whole relationship consisted of trading e-mails and instant messages and syrupy comments on each other's home pages. She was too scared to commit to a real-world F2F encounter yet. They'd never even spoken on the phone—he'd suggested it once, but she deflected it out of nerves.

Not that she had anything to worry about. She was certain he was three-name cute, even though he didn't have any pics on his profile—just a cute *Speed Racer* cartoon. She just had a *feeling*. A. A. liked to think she was a little bit psychic, and she could *sense* a hot boy behind those sweet e-mails. He'd already changed his profile to "In a Relationship" ever since they'd confessed their affection to each other a week ago. He kept telling her he couldn't wait until they met for real.

And there lay the problem. They could never meet for real.

Because laxjock (his online handle) was a high school boy. Who thought she was four years older than she really was.

If only she really were sixteen years old like it said on her profile! She'd kind of fudged with her age on the site, everyone did. Who in their right mind wanted to admit they were in junior high? Duh. In her defense, the stunning, professional black-and-white portrait on her page certainly made her *look* sixteen.

Her mother, a former model who had walked the catwalks of Paris, Milan, and New York, had asked a famous fashion photographer to take shots of her daughter as a favor, and the resulting photograph—of A. A. in a sleek black Eres bikini—was totally *Teen Vogue*—worthy.

Although the photo was sort of a fluke, really. A. A. had always been a bit of a tomboy, and she was most comfortable in Puma sneakers and yoga pants. It always bothered her that all her life she'd been taller than everyone she knew, had filled out the earliest, had gotten her first bra *years* before her friends had.

It was embarrassing how people were always commenting on how she looked older than her real age, how she looked "more mature." Was there ever a word more depressing than "mature"? A. A. thought "mature" meant a wheelchair, a nursing home, and sensible shoes with the crepe wedges. She'd always hated looking older than she was. Until she had turned twelve years old but looked sixteen—then suddenly the world opened up in all sorts of delicious ways, like being able to sneak into R-rated movies and all-ages teen nightclubs.

She figured she would just delay their meeting until she was sure he was so in love with her that he wouldn't care that she was only in seventh grade. Right?

"Loverboy?" Ashley asked, noticing A. A. putting her phone away.

"It's her online Romeo," added Lili with a knowing smile.

"Yeah." A. A. sighed, trying not to look too pleased.

"So when do we get to meet him already?" Lili asked impatiently. "We've been hearing about him for weeks. Time to give up the goods."

"Soon," A. A. said airily. She had yet to confess to her friends that she herself had never met him. Some things were best kept secret for a while.

"You're so mysterious about him, maybe he doesn't really exist," Ashley teased.

A. A. shrugged, knowing they couldn't help but be just a tiny bit jealous she had boy drama in her life. For all of Ashley's sophistication, she had yet to kiss a boy. Lili swore up and down that she'd kissed a boy over the summer in Taiwan, but with no way to prove it, she got only dubious credit for the experience.

Whereas she, A. A., had already made out with not one but two boys—last year her older cousin had taken her to a high school party and she'd made out with two Saint Aloysius freshmen during a game of Truth/Dare/Double Dare/Promise to Repeat. One of them had even stalked her for weeks, even after finding out she was only eleven.

He was cute, but a little demented. She finally had to get her cousin to tell him to buzz off.

"Yeah, sure, A. A. has a boyfriend—but only she can see him!" Ashley teased. "It's like *The Sixth Sense.*"

"An imaginary boyfriend, how cute!" Lili laughed condescendingly. "They must have lots to say to each other."

"Shut up!" A. A. said, flicking Lili on the shoulder.

"Owww." Lili pouted. "That hurt."

A. A. briefly wondered what her life would be like if her parents had named her Samantha, like they had originally planned. She knew Lili was still peeved about Ashley's handbag switcheroo. A. A. wasn't thrilled about it either, but she had known better than to complain about it.

Whatever. It was the first day of school. Seventh grade. Finally. Boy-girl dances. Coed parties. Free-dress Fridays. It was going to rock.

School was just a few steps away, and A. A. could sense her friends subconsciously starting to move at slow-motion speed, and she did the same, savoring the feeling of having all eyes on them. Lili began to toss her long dark hair back over her shoulder in an exaggerated shampoo-commercial way, while Ashley pursed her lips as if preparing for a camera close-up. A. A. walked a little taller, arching her back and keeping her arm swing to a minimum.

They sat on the bench by the playground, where they could check out everyone and make judgments on new back-to-school haircuts and sock choices. There was very little room to make a fashion statement with the uniform (or as A. A. called it, the prison outfit), so every variation was scrutinized to death, from skirt hemline—rolled up to super mini length was totally out and way too much like the slutty Helena Academy girls down the street—to necklace choice: points for the Tiffany bean, negatory on jelly necklaces.

"Skiddoo," Ashley growled at a couple of first graders who'd had the unfortunate idea to play hopscotch in front of the bench.

A. A. took her customary place on Ashley's right, Lili on Ashley's left, the three of them sitting cross-legged, kicking their ankles high so everyone could take note of their matching red-soled Louboutin Mary Janes, whispering to one another as girls from their class walked by. Those in their favor stopped and said hello, while those beneath notice scurried by with their heads bowed low, hoping to escape criticism. No such luck.

"Nice jacket," Ashley sneered, as Daria Hart, a fashion-challenged seventh grader, walked by in a metallic raincoat. "It'll come in handy when the aliens land."

Lili giggled, while A. A. gave Daria what she hoped was

a she-didn't-really-mean-it smile. Ashley could be pretty funny, and A. A. enjoyed a cutting comment as much as anyone, but A. A. was feeling less and less inclined to be mean just for meanness' sake.

Melody Myers, an SOA, stopped to trade what-I-did-last-summer stories and oohed over their matching Prada charms. As Melody hurried away when the first bell rang, a shiny silver Bentley pulled up to the sidewalk in front of the school. The girls didn't give it a second look—expensive cars were a typical sight in the mornings at Miss Gamble's—but the hot guy climbing out of the front seat definitely caught their attention.

He was tall and chiseled, with a cool buzz cut, and he wore a pair of silver wraparound sunglasses. When he opened the back door, his biceps flexed in a most heart-stopping manner. A. A. couldn't take her eyes off him.

Then a pair of tanned legs wearing last year's chunky socks and brand-new high-heeled black-and-white spectators emerged, as a girl none of them had ever seen before got out of the car. She was so pretty it almost hurt to look at her. Perfect hair. Perfect skin. Perfect nose. A Fendi Moncler bag, in the much more expensive silver snakeskin that was sold out at Neiman's, was hanging on her shoulder.

Too bad about the socks. Ashley had decreed chunky

socks passé, and all of them were wearing black tights that morning.

A. A. raised an eyebrow. She looked at Ashley's and Lili's blank faces and knew what they were thinking. Here was a girl pretty enough to steal the Ashleys' thunder. Did she know what she was in for?

The girl walked by with her nose in the air, completely ignoring them, as if they didn't matter. Nobody said a word. Then Ashley stuck out her foot. A. A. gasped inwardly. It was the oldest trick in the book. But here was the thing about old tricks: They worked.

For a split second it looked like the new girl would be able to catch herself before connecting with Ashley's outstretched ankle, but there would be no such salvation that day. She went flailing on her Chanel pumps, tumbling to the ground as the contents of her designer handbag spilled, showering books and notebooks and pencil case everywhere, and her skirt flew up to her waist, revealing baggy Carter's underwear. Not so perfect after all.

"Oops." Ashley giggled. "I'm *so* sorry," she said, not sounding the least bit apologetic.

The girl brushed her bangs away from her face, and A. A. suddenly recognized her, as did her friends.

"Omigod. It's Lauren Page," said Lili in a shocked tone.

"Who?" Ashley sniffed. "Never mind."

"You should really watch where you're going," A. A. cautioned.

"Yeah, try not to bump into my foot next time. You almost gave me a bruise," Ashley added.

Then, without another word, the Ashleys stood up from the bench, climbed daintily over Lauren's sprawled body, and walked into school.

5

BUT ISN'T IMITATION THE SINCEREST FORM OF FLATTERY?

"WHAT'S THAT?" LAUREN'S MOM asked right before ringing the doorbell to the Spencers' grand home, pointing to a thin red scratch on Lauren's right cheek.

"It's nothing. Accident at gym." Lauren shook her head. The fall had been completely humiliating, and she was still a little stunned at how deftly the Ashleys had been able to derail her plan before it had even begun. But it could have been worse. There could have been an audience. Luckily, it had happened after the second bell rang, and the only person who had witnessed her social disaster was the elderly school custodian, who'd been kind enough to help her up.

Lauren kept a low profile for the rest of the day. She avoided her old friends—if you could call them that, since they had nothing in common other than the fact that they were shunned by the rest of the class: Cass Franklin, who was allergic to everything and kept an inhaler and an oxygen tank in her bag in case of emergency; and Guinevere Parker, whom everyone called Bobblehead because her head was much too large for her way-too-skinny body.

She had been so sure that her new look would get her immediately seated at the Ashleys' table at lunch, but since it was glaringly apparent that that was not going to happen anytime soon, she'd decided to skip it entirely and hid in the library eating her cheese panini until it was over. She'd heard a few whispers about her transformation but had ignored the friendly overtures from some of the other girls in class. Sheridan Riley was particularly effusive—fawning over Lauren's shiny hair and new bag when she had hardly paid any attention to her before. But Lauren had been at Miss Gamble's long enough to know that the only opinion that mattered was the Ashleys'. She didn't want to settle for anything less.

Trudy Page looked at her daughter keenly, licking her finger and rubbing the wound. "Are you sure that's all it was?"

"Mom, stop. Okay?" Lauren pleaded, flinching away. "I promise you, it was nothing."

Trudy sighed. She adjusted the thick braided Gucci belt around her silk tunic and wild paisley-print palazzo pants.

Lauren couldn't help but notice that ever since the company had gone public, her mother had begun to dress very loudly. Money talks, and apparently, so does Cavalli.

Lauren had changed out of her uniform and was wearing a bib-front Chloé minidress and ankle-strap wedges. Her new personal shopper assured her it was the hottest new look of the season, and even though the shoes pinched her feet, Lauren didn't complain. When she was one of the Ashleys, it would all be worth it. Especially when she stomped all over them.

After that morning's incident, she decided to change tactics. She'd been such a dummy. Of course her Extreme Makeover wouldn't be enough to entice the Ashleys to become her friend. And she had to befriend them first, otherwise how would she ever learn how to take them down? So it was time for a more direct approach: Operation Kiss-Up.

Trudy rang the bell again just as the Spencers' butler, a white-haired gentleman in a crisp morning suit, opened the door with a polite nod.

"Good afternoon," he greeted them. "May I take your coats and contribution?"

Lauren took off her brand-new fur-trimmed Chloé windbreaker, while Trudy handed over her hot pink Burberry trench. The mother-daughter welcome back tea had been instituted just last year at Miss Gamble's, and some well-meaning souls on the Mothers Committee had decided that it would be potluck. The idea was to make the tea more democratic, since it was more than obvious that any of the Miss Gamble's parents could easily have provided a four-course spread on their own, complete with cater-waiters and valet parking.

As it was, whoever hosted the tea provided the catered spread anyway, and the potluck aspect merely served to highlight the vast chasm between the scholarship students and the legacy kids.

Last year Trudy had brought homemade picnic sandwiches to the tea at Ashley Li's house and, to their supreme embarrassment, discovered that a Miss Gamble's potluck meant that everyone had brought miniature French pastries and tea sandwiches from chic Nob Hill gourmet shops. Lauren had been utterly devastated upon encountering the tiny squares of smoked salmon and minute cucumber wedges. They never did find out what happened to those four sad turkey sandwiches, and the two of them had never discussed it.

This time, instead of handing over a sagging brown bag, Trudy proudly gestured to a portly Englishman wearing chef's whites who followed behind them. "This is Graham," she said. "Can you show him and his staff the kitchen, please?"

The chef and his crew lugged overstuffed grocery bags bearing the logo of the city's premier gourmet grocery, as well as a towering structure that was a scale-size replica of the school's main building. To compensate for last year's faux pas, Trudy had flown in a private chef from one of London's best restaurants to concoct authentic and delicious English treats. And just in case that wasn't impressive enough, she'd thrown in a massive chocolate fountain based on the school's architecture as well.

To Lauren's mother's disappointment, the Spencers' butler didn't look at all surprised and ushered the Pages into the sunroom and Graham and his workers to the kitchen without comment.

Lauren had never been in Ashley Spencer's house before, and she looked around eagerly, as if the sun-dappled walls would provide a clue as to how to make Ashley like her more. They walked past the marble entryway into the light-filled great room with a CinemaScope view of the Golden Gate Bridge and the blue waters of San Francisco Bay.

Last year the two of them had been intimidated by the Li family's lavish home, but this time they hardly blinked at seeing the Picasso hanging above the grand piano. After all, they now owned two of the great master's works themselves. However, Lauren couldn't help but notice that the Spencers' view of the bridge was just a little nicer than theirs.

"Trudy! Lauren! Welcome!" Matilda Spencer said, graciously receiving them with her customary warmth. Ashley's mom was dressed in a simple linen sheath, a lustrous pearl necklace as her only accessory. She looked stunning.

Lauren could never understand how Ashley could be so mean when her mom was just so *nice*. She probably didn't even realize that her daughter was a beast from hell.

"Ashley, come say hi to our guests," called Matilda.

The three of them waited patiently for Ashley to say hello. When she finally made her way to her mother's side, Lauren's only thought was, *Oh, no.*

Ashley was wearing the same exact bib-front Chloé dress and ankle-strap platforms.

Lauren watched Ashley's expression change from indifference to horror upon seeing her. She was sure Ashley's head would explode.

Thinking fast, before Ashley could say anything, Lauren gave her a big, bone-crushing hug. "Cute outfit, Ashley! I wish I looked as good as you do in it! I know it's all wrong for me, but it looks killer on you."

"Really?" Ashley asked, pinking. Her shoulders relaxed. "It looks cute on you, too," she said graciously.

Lauren exhaled. Okay. If Ashley Spencer was this easy to please, maybe there was still hope.

6

DON'T MESS WITH THE QUEEN
OF PARLOR GAMES

COULD LIFE BE EVEN MORE UNFAIR? This was not how it was supposed to go down. You'd think that after the welcome splat they'd given her that morning, this Lauren chick would get the message. So what if her dad had become some kind of Internet gazillionaire like everyone in class was saying? And okay, so maybe Lauren was now really pretty. Even Ashley had to grudgingly admit that the girl was like some sort of Rachel Bilson clone.

But c'mon, this was Lauren Page they were talking about—in kindergarten the Ashleys had made her eat mud! Every day! Until Lauren's mom had finally complained to the school that her daughter was coming home with strange stomach pains, and they had to stop. Things just didn't change around Miss

Gamble's. There were those on top and those at the bottom, and that was how it was. Everyone knew their place. Otherwise the whole system could come crashing down.

And now this!

The back-to-school tea was supposed to be all about debuting *her* new look. She'd picked out the Chloé dress especially for its unique design, and to see Lauren wearing it was, like, more than blasphemous. Her thunder was totally stolen.

Ashley stood with a huge fake smile plastered to her face as her mother made nice with Lauren's scary mom. Someone should tell that lady that zebra print, leopard print, and paisley should never, ever be worn all at the same time. When Matilda finally led Lauren's mom away, Ashley abruptly turned on her heel and walked quickly back to her friends. She made it clear that she didn't expect Lauren to follow her, but Lauren kept up anyway, matching her stride for stride.

The Ashleys were seated in a prime spot by the window. Lili was sipping carefully from her teacup, while A. A. was playing with Princess Dahlia von Fluffsterhaus, Ashley's labradoodle puppy. They both looked up when they saw Ashley and Lauren.

Lili gasped. "Twins!" she squealed, beginning to laugh. But she quickly cupped her hand over her mouth when she saw the death-ray look on Ashley's face.

"I know. We're, like, separated at birth!" Lauren joked, brazenly taking a seat next to A. A. on the floor as if she had always been in their inner circle.

"If only." Ashley smiled thinly, knowing she would have to continue to pretend that the whole debacle didn't bother her in the least, although now that she was pretending to be so chummy, it looked like they had *planned* to wear the same clothes on purpose. As if they were friends or something. Hello.

"Cute puppy! Can I hold him?" asked Lauren, looking nervous.

A. A. looked at Ashley, who shrugged. Let Lauren play with Princess Dahlia. Maybe if she was lucky Princess Dahlia would bite her.

Ashley knew that the other girls at the tea were beginning to notice that Lauren was seated with them. Now everyone would think that the Ashleys liked Lauren, when nothing could be further from the truth.

She licked her teaspoon and watched Lauren laugh with A. A. while they played with the puppy. This had to stop. She could smell an interloper a mile away. In fourth grade, Kennedy Taylor had tried the same thing—to join the Ashleys. She had the complete set of Bratz dolls and thought that was all it took.

But if anyone could be an Ashley, then what was the point

of being an Ashley? Kennedy had to transfer schools after the Ashleys were through with her.

Somehow Ashley got the feeling Lauren wouldn't be so easy to get rid of. She would have to take the matter in hand immediately.

"I'm bored!" Ashley announced, putting down her teacup with a clatter on the coffee table. She bit her cuticle and looked around the pale paneled room, with its fluted columns and crystal vases filled with abundant bouquets. Some big fat guy in chef's whites was passing out a tray of hors d'oeuvres to the oohs and aahs of the assembled guests. Her mother was still greeting new arrivals by the entrance, playing with the string of pearls around her neck and trying to look interested in what Suki Atwater-Smith's mother had to say.

"I call Truth or Dare," she finally decided. "Who's in?"

A. A. and Lili perked up, while Lauren looked slightly anxious. Good.

She decided to start off slowly. "Lili."

"Dare," said Lili, tossing her glossy curls over one shoulder and looking game for anything Ashley had in mind.

"I dare you to kiss Princess Dahlia on the lips," Ashley said with a grin, knowing that Lili wasn't too fond of animals.

Lili rolled her eyes, scrunched up her face, and gave the puppy a quick smack on the lips. "Done," she said. She daintily wiped her lips with a Kleenex. "Puppy cooties, eww."

"Princess Dahlia is cleaner than you!" Ashley retorted, picking up the dog and kissing her on the lips as well. "Pick your victim."

Lili pointed a breadstick in A. A.'s direction, but put it down before eating it. "A. A. What'll it be?"

"Truth," A. A. said cheerfully.

"Do you stuff your bra?" Lili asked quickly, so it was obvious it was a question she'd been meaning to ask A. A. for some time now.

Ashley snorted. "Lil, that's so lame. We all know A. A. is rolling Cs," she said, noticing A. A. hug herself tightly so no one could look at her chest. "Do-over," she ordered.

"Fine," Lili huffed. "Truth again?"

A. A. mulled it over. "I'll take a dare this time," she mumbled.

Ashley whispered in Lili's ear, and when she pulled away Lili had a slightly mocking smile on her face. "I dare you to text your boyfriend you love him," she said. All the while, Ashley noticed that Lauren was hunched over her teacup, trying to make herself as inconspicuous as possible.

"Do I have to?" groaned A. A.

"You know the rules," Ashley reminded her gleefully.

A. A. sighed, took out her phone, and began to type. "Okaaaay. God, I hope he doesn't think I'm some kind of stalker!" she said, putting away her iPhone.

She turned to Ashley. "Your turn!"

"Dare," Ashley said, knowing that A. A. thought up the least exciting dares. Sure enough, A. A. came through. "I dare you to yell 'Miss Gamble's sucks!' right now," A. A. ordered.

"Easy," Ashley mocked. "Watch this." She threw her head back and yelled, "MISS GAMBLE'S SUCKS!" to the surprise of the room. Spoons clattered to the floor. Her mother shot her a look, but she shrugged it off.

"Done," she said. "Now it's my turn to choose." Ashley looked intently at the three girls. She loved this part—the anticipation on her friends' faces, the barely disguised anxiety on Lauren's. Ashley prided herself on thinking up the most revealing questions and the most impossible dares. Last time they'd played, Lili had to walk around at the mall with her skirt tucked into her underwear and toilet paper hanging out, and A. A. had to moon a bus filled with Gregory Hall boys. A picture of A. A.'s butt was still floating around in cyberspace.

"Lauren," she finally decided, zeroing in on the intruder in their midst. "Truth or dare?"

"Dare?" Lauren asked tentatively, with a nervous smile frozen on her face.

"Good choice." Ashley got up and walked through the room, pausing to smile at a few mothers on her way out of the party.

"Uh, bye," said A. A. as she looked at Lili. "Totally random."

Ashley smiled to herself. If Lauren thought her dare would be as easy as kissing a dog, she had another thing coming. And then she was back, holding out her hand to Lauren. On her palm were a few dark clumps. "I dare you to drop these into the chocolate fountain," she said.

"What? Why?" asked Lauren, giggling nervously.

"Because I dared you, duh," Ashley snapped.

"What are they?" Lauren asked.

"Poisonous mushrooms grounded up. I've been saving them for a special occasion. Oh, don't look at me like that, A. A. They're not going to kill anyone. These are pretty benign. All they'll do is make a few people throw up."

"C'mon it'll be funny," Lili cooed.

"No, it won't," muttered Lauren, picking up the puppy and holding her so close that they couldn't see her face.

"You could call a double dare," put in A. A. helpfully. "But I wouldn't, since Ashley's double dares are even worse than her dares. And if you take a 'Promise to Repeat,' you can postpone it, but then you'd have to do it twice in the future."

"Either way, you're just making it worse, really," Lili pointed out.

"And if you forfeit a dare, you have to do whatever we tell you for a whole week. Those are the rules," Ashley declared.

"And we all have *tons* of homework, don't we, girls?"

"Tons." A. A. nodded. Ashley wasn't kidding. Miss Gamble's was one of the top academic institutions in the city, and everyone obsessed over ISEE scores, which were mandatory for prep school admission.

"Gee, and it would be nice if someone could get us lunch from Gino's Deli every day too. I'm so tired of brown-bagging," Lili agreed.

"You don't want to have to fetch our lunch every day, do you, Lauren?" asked Ashley sweetly.

Lauren paled. She put the dog down, snatched the mushrooms from Ashley's hand, and slowly walked over to the chocolate fountain.

Ashley watched her go with satisfaction. No one ever dared turn down a dare. After Lauren put the mushrooms in, she would make her eat some chocolate from the fountain. This was even more fun than kindergarten.

7

SO THIS IS HOW RUMORS
GET STARTED

WHILE LAUREN WENT TO SABOTAGE her mother's precious chocolate fountain, Ashley motioned to her friends to put their heads together. It was decision time, Lili knew. She had been wondering how long Ashley would let that charade last. Poor Lauren, why did she even try? Ashley never made new friends. She was like a barracuda. All teeth.

"She seems okay," A. A. ventured, cuddling Princess Dahlia. A. A. said that about everybody.

"A. A., have you lost your mind? She's a total zero. She'll always be a total zero," Ashley said vehemently, stretching forward so her elbows were balanced on her knees.

"She's a zero who's wearing your dress," Lili reminded her, taking a strawberry tart from the three-tiered dessert tray on the coffee table, then putting it down, untouched, on her plate after noticing that neither of her friends was eating anything. Her stomach grumbled, but she'd have to wait to eat till she got home.

"Shut up," said Ashley, annoyed. She looked to the other side of the room and watched intently as Lauren slipped the mushroom dust into the molten chocolate pool.

"Don't tell me to shut up!" Lili complained.

"Shut up!" Ashley yelled again. She was so impossible sometimes, Lili thought, although she was temporarily mollified when Ashley gave her a playful swat on the arm to show she was kidding. Ashley motioned the other girls to move closer so they wouldn't be overheard, but before she could lay down her verdict, Sheridan Riley came over to say hello.

Lili didn't like Sheridan Riley very much. Even though Sheridan was an SOA, Lili had no patience for Sheridan's crew. They blatantly worshipped the Ashleys and wanted nothing more than to be like them. Unfortunately, Sheridan had too-short bangs and a tendency to spit when she talked. Plus, her name was Sheridan. And on parents' days her mom and dad wore matching Burberry outfits.

"Hey, guys. Did I just see you hanging out with Lauren Page?" Sheridan asked, getting immediately to the point.

"Yeah, we have to be nice to her. She's had *such* a hard life," Ashley said, her voice dripping with concern. She pulled out a pot of lip balm from her bag and began to apply a thick smear on her lips. "Medex?" she offered.

"Really?" Sheridan asked, slouching down to sit on the window bench next to Lili while she reached over and stuck her finger right into the center, making a huge dent in the wax. Lili saw Ashley grimace. You were supposed to dab lightly.

"I heard the total opposite. Her dad is, like, the head of YourTV.com and they're worth, like, billions. Plus I heard Lauren's going to have her own reality series on Nickelodeon," Sheridan told them as she carefully applied the balm to her chapped lips.

Lili recoiled, and she could see her friends chafe at that revelation as well. Lauren Page, television star? Now that was a blow. Usually only the Ashleys were the subjects of such celebrated gossip. Lauren's makeover was way more successful than they had given her credit for. Lili wondered what Ashley would do about it and wasn't surprised when Ashley motioned Sheridan closer.

"Keep it," Ashley said, waving away the lip balm Sheridan held out. "Now, I don't like to say stuff about people, but I heard something about Lauren's family," she said, in her most self-righteous voice. Lili was always impressed at how Ashley was able to preface her catty comments with a goody-goody disclaimer so that she wouldn't look too snotty, and somehow, it always worked.

Sheridan looked eagerly at Ashley, waiting to hear whatever rumor she might be about to reveal.

"You're not going to tell anybody, right?" Ashley asked.

Sheridan shook her head and made an X sign above her chest. The girl lived to spread dirt on everyone.

Ashley sighed as if it broke her heart to disclose what she was about to say. She motioned the girls even closer. "It's all Mafia money." She looked at Lili and A. A. to back her up, and both girls nodded in agreement.

"Serious?" Sheridan asked, eyes wide, lapping up every word.

"Serious."

"Huge crime family," A. A. added wisely. "Like the Sopranos? But worse."

"And that makeover? It's so sad," said Lili, deciding it was time to get in on the game. "It's a cry for help."

"Why? She looks so cute! I wish I had her nose," Sheridan said, touching her huge honker.

"If you did, you'd be a pigface too." Lili told her somberly. An idea was starting to form in her head. This was so wrong, but she couldn't help herself, especially when she saw the grin beginning to spread on Ashley's face.

"What do you mean?" asked Sheridan, her face flushed and eager. She craned her neck to look across the room, watching Lauren walk back toward them.

"You know how they use pig organs now in surgery?" Lili asked, as if imparting some really important information. She pulled her hair back behind her ears and looked Sheridan in the eye. "Doctors putting pig livers and pig hearts in people?"

Sheridan nodded. "Yeah, I've heard of that."

"Well, they do it in plastic surgery now too. Let's just say that Lauren has a new *snout*," Lili revealed. Then she pinched her nose and made an oinking noise.

Sheridan looked from one Ashley to another. "You're joking. She got a nose job? No way." This was even better than when they told her about Melody Myers peeing in her pants during the sixth-grade field trip. They called Melody "Peezilla" and "The Princess and the Pee" for weeks.

"Way." Ashley nodded vigorously, pointing to her own slim button nose. "The tip? One hundred percent pork."

A. A. snorted into her teacup. *Control yourself, A. A.*, Lili thought.

"Omigod." Sheridan started giggling uncontrollably. She was still laughing when she walked across the room to tell her friends what the Ashleys had just told her.

Lili smiled at her friends. Pigface Mafia Princess. Priceless. Of course, it was so outrageous it couldn't possibly be true. But try telling that to the gossip-mad girls at Miss Gamble's.

49

When Lauren returned, the three of them were doubled over, clutching their stomachs in laughter.

"What's so funny?" she asked, looking at the other girls.

"Nothing," said Ashley, the very picture of angelic virtue.

Lili didn't meet Lauren's eye. It was one thing to make fun of someone when they were across the room, but a totally different story when they were sitting right in front of you. Looking so hopelessly *eager*.

Then A. A. accidentally snorted while sipping her tea, and the three of them began laughing again.

By the time the tea was over, Lili knew that no one would even care how rich Lauren was supposed to be, or how good she looked. Because who could be jealous of a little Miss Piggy?

8

A PRIVATE TEA PARTY

ASHLEY'S HOUSE WAS ONLY A FEW DOORS down from her place, so A. A. lingered, helping clean up—which meant hanging out with Ashley and her mom at the Spencers' kitchen counter while the kitchen staff did all the dirty work. This was A. A.'s favorite part of any party, when all the guests were gone and only a few close friends remained and everyone could relax and unwind and get down to the real business of eating. Too bad Lili couldn't stay longer, but her mom was always ridiculously strict about her "timetable" and kept Lili on a rigid schedule. She'd marched Lili right home for violin practice.

"Well, that was a success, don't you think?" Matilda Spencer asked, hands on her hips as she surveyed the copious remains of the tea. "Nancy always orders too much food, and with Trudy bringing in her whole entourage, we had enough to feed an army."

"Yeah, Mom, you rocked it," said Ashley, bumping her mother on the hip while opening the door to the Sub-Zero. She brought out a whole tray of gourmet tea sandwiches, a tub of chocolate pudding, and assorted cream puffs and pastries, and laid everything out on the island counter in front of them.

"Ooh, yum," A. A. said happily, rubbing her hands with glee at all the bounty.

"Dibs on the éclairs," Ashley warned, reaching for a gooey chocolate-covered treat. "Suzanne makes the best ones," she added, referring to their cook.

A. A. waved her off. Ashley could keep the éclairs. They weren't even made of real chocolate, and they tasted like cardboard—everything at the Spencers' was carob this and yogurt that. Instead she grabbed one of the golden brown scones nestled underneath a folded linen napkin in a silver bowl. "You can have them. These are my favorite. Mmm. They're still warm!"

"Can you believe they flew him all the way out just for the tea to bake those?" Ashley asked, as she wiped dark brown icing from her lips with a monogrammed napkin. "Someone's insecure."

"Hey, if they want to throw their money around, that's fine with me," said A. A., spreading clotted cream on her scone and putting the entire thing into her mouth.

"Girls, be nice," Matilda warned, picking up a cherry tomato from a crudités platter. "They just wanted to make an effort. I'm sure she was just embarrassed about last year."

"What happened last year?" Ashley asked, looking up from her second éclair, a chocolate mustache on her lip. "I don't remember anything."

A. A. devoured three scones in short order while Ashley's mom told them about Lauren's mom's sad turkey sandwiches.

"We had to give them to the homeless. I didn't want them to go to waste." Matilda sighed.

Ashley shot her a look, and A. A. snickered. Okay, so it was totally mean to laugh at someone's social faux pas, but seriously. Picnic sandwiches? Even her mom, who was in Barbados with some senator during last year's tea, had managed to send their maid over with a box of Italian cookies.

"Pass that cheese plate," she requested, pointing to an oval platter stacked with five different kinds of artisanal cheese. A. A. wasn't a secret eater like Ashley was, but she did relax knowing her mom wasn't around to tell her to eat like a lady. Meanwhile, Ashley, who was on, like, a tissue diet in public, was a total hog in private. The girl had such a complex she never even let Lili see her eat. Those two were way too competitive.

A. A. counted herself lucky. She lived on ice cream and hamburgers every day and never gained any weight.

"Did you see her face when Sheridan's mom announced that there was something wrong with the chocolate in the fountain?" Ashley asked, piling her plate high with totally tasteless gluten-free potato salad and organic crème fraîche squares.

A. A. nodded. It had been pretty funny. Trudy Page had been totally offended and had eaten a huge dollop of melted chocolate on a slice of pound cake. A few minutes later, she was clutching her stomach and hurrying Lauren out the door. The other mothers had quickly pronounced the fountain off-limits. Sometimes you had to hand it to Ashley. She knew how to make things exciting.

"Yes, wasn't that odd?" Ashley's mom mused, playing with her pearls and picking up a stick of celery. "I never trust those things." She shuddered. "All that chocolate just melting there . . . it's a haven for bacteria. I can never understand why people get so excited about them. They're so tacky."

Ashley smirked, and A. A. coughed into her hand.

"Well, I'm full," Ashley's mom announced, after having eaten, from what A. A. could tell, two pieces of vegetables. "I can't possibly eat dinner."

A. A. bet that Ashley's mom was just like her mom, subsisting on tidbits and vitamin supplements instead of real food. Her mom always told her that one day she wouldn't be able to eat the way she did, and A. A. hoped for her own sake

54

that that day would never come. "Scone?" she asked, offering Ashley the silver bowl.

Ashley looked longingly at the buttery biscuit. Her mother paused, looking back at her daughter. Then Ashley quickly shook her head. "Carbs? Uh-uh."

"More for me." A. A. shrugged as she finished off the last of the golden brown pastries. She could never understand why anyone would deprive themselves of the good things in life.

9

MTV ISN'T THE ONLY ONE WITH PARENTAL CONTROL

ILI WISHED HER MOM WOULD HAVE LET THEM stay longer, but there was no arguing with her mother's wishes. Her parents were convinced that if she tried hard enough, she would be another Sarah Chang—the Korean-American child prodigy who was one of the top violinists in the world before she turned eighteen. Violin was the least of it—Lili was signed up for a ton of after-school activities that were tailored to fit her mother's idea of a well-rounded Ivy League—bound profile, even though college was light-years away.

On the schedule: community service—and not mere candy-striping, but assisting a genetic researcher at Stanford; foreign language fluency in French, German, and Mandarin; art appreciation—black-and-white still photography lessons with a renowned artist, as well as becoming the youngest-ever docent at the de Young museum.

Any other kid might have buckled under the weight of so much expectation, so much parental pressure. Luckily enough, Lili was good at everything. It all came easily to her—too easily, maybe. She had a talent for being "talented." And since it came easily, Lili could care less about any of her accomplishments. Her mother wanted her to grow up to be a combination of Miss America, Wonder Woman, and Hillary Clinton. But Lili had bigger dreams.

When she grew up, she wanted to move to New York and run a nightclub.

Not that she'd ever been to one, but it sure sounded like a lot of fun. Lili liked having fun, especially since fun was not something you could "schedule."

It sucked that she had to leave the tea, since it meant she would miss out on something important as usual, because Lili guessed that when she wasn't there, A. A. and Ashley talked about her, just as when Ashley didn't join them for tennis on Saturdays, she and A. A. spent the day gossiping about her, and on Tuesdays and Thursdays when A. A. had a different lunch period, she and Ashley spent the hour picking her apart.

She sat quietly in the back of her mother's black hybrid SUV as their driver drove them back to their house in

Presidio Heights, just a few blocks away. Like Pacific Heights, it was an exclusive, affluent neighborhood filled with beautiful homes and immaculate gardens.

"That was nice, wasn't it?" asked her mother.

"Uh-huh," Lili replied softly, tracing a finger on the windowpane and making smiley faces in the mist.

"Was that Lauren Page I saw you girls with earlier?" her mother continued, removing a Chanel compact from her bag and powdering her nose.

Lili nodded, feeling a small twinge of guilt at making up that ridiculous story about Lauren. Already people were oinking whenever they saw the poor girl running to and from the bathroom after Ashley's second dare.

But whatever, the girl should be old enough to take care of herself, right? It wasn't Lili's fault—it was just a *joke*.

"It's nice that you guys are making new friends," Nancy said, snapping the case shut as they arrived at the gates of their palatial Tudor mansion.

"Mmm," replied Lili, wondering if her mother had any idea of what had really happened at the tea. Winston, their chauffeur, opened the back door for them, and she got out of the car quickly before her mother could ask her any more about it.

When they walked in, their chef was already making dinner, and a delicious smell was emanating from the oven.

Lili's twin three-year-old sisters, Josephine and Brennan, were running around like banshees, wet blue paint on their hands, their nannies running after them with towels. Her mother's two personal assistants were buzzing around with wireless receivers strapped to their ears. One was going through a thick stack of invitations, while the other was faxing replies.

Her two older sisters were away, one at college and the other at boarding school. Lili missed them more than she thought she would. Her older sisters had teased and tormented her mercilessly, but now she wished more than anything that they still lived at home.

Her mother had quit her job to be with her family, but it seemed she was busier than ever. There was always so much activity in the house. Sometimes Lili felt it was more of an office than a home, and she was merely a junior associate in her mother's old law firm. Someone who was expected to execute deliverables.

"What's this?" Nancy asked, noticing a yellow slip sticking out of one of Lili's books on the counter. It was the late notice from this morning. "You were late? But I dropped you off at the corner at seven thirty."

"I met Ashley at Starbucks first. I blame the baristas. It took them so long to make our lattes," Lili joked, steeling herself for a lecture as her mother read the note and frowned.

Sure enough, Nancy put a hand on her daughter's shoulder and crouched down so she could look her in the eye. She folded up the note, and it was obvious from her brisk demeanor that she knew what had happened. Lili was never late unless Ashley was involved somehow. "Sweetie, you know I adore Ashley, but she has too much of an influence on you," her mother said.

Ever since Lili had brought home a "warning" from the headmistress's office after the SOA sticker caper, Nancy had gotten it into her head that the Ashleys were nothing but trouble, and the late notice didn't help any.

"You really have to learn to be your own person," her mother said firmly. "Get out of her shadow."

Lili tried not to show her annoyance, since it would land her in more hot water. But how exactly did you become your own person when you shared the same name with the two most popular girls in your class?

10

JUST ONE OF THE GUYS?

A.A. LIVED IN A PENTHOUSE APARTMENT ON top of the Fairmont Hotel in the middle of Nob Hill (also known in more resentful quarters as "Snob Hill"). She had lived there all her life. Her mother had fled New York and repaired to a two-bedroom suite when she was getting a divorce from her second ex-husband, a British rock star, and had never checked out. Instead she had upgraded, taking over the entire floor with money from the settlement. Upon arriving in San Francisco, she quickly met and married A. A.'s dad, the former mayor of the city, but divorced him a few years ago. Her mother still traveled constantly, and A. A. was never quite sure where she was or if she would be there when she got home.

The only constant in her life was her older half brother Zed Starlight, whose father was the ex-rocker her mother had left upon finding out he had not one but four love children with assorted groupies all over the globe. Zed had changed his name to Ned Alioto after A. A.'s dad pretty much adopted him when he married their mom. Ned never saw his real dad except on VH1 nostalgia shows, and he told A. A. he was tired of being the kid with the funny name.

Ned was hanging out in the suite's plush living room with a couple of his friends from school when she got home. They were nice enough boys, although completely obsessed with video games. Ned and his posse were on all the important sports teams at Gregory Hall, but A. A. never heard them talk about anything except what games they owned, what games they planned to buy, what games had secret shortcut codes that allowed you to get to the final levels, and whether it was time to order pizza.

Two of the guys were battling it out onscreen, brandishing Wii sticks like automatic weapons while the rest watched intently.

"Get him! Over there! Turn the corner and—"

"I'm—aaah . . . !"

"Take that!" Slaps and tapped fists all around as a zombie's head exploded in a burst of green goo.

"Can I have next game?" A. A. asked, squinting at the screen and sitting on the nearest empty chaise. Might as well join in the fun.

"Sure," one of the boys agreed, tossing one of the four controllers her way. A. A. lined up her shots and racked up a huge score in seconds. "You suck, Fitzpatrick," she taunted, tossing the joystick back into the pile.

"Suck this, Alioto," responded the boy who'd lost to her, flipping her off with a grin.

A. A. pulled a face. Boys were such doofuses. Sometimes she wondered what girls ever saw in them. From what she could see from her brother and his friends, all they wanted to do was play video games until their brains turned to mush.

Of course, laxjock wasn't like that at all. He was a real gentleman. Yesterday he even removed a virus on her profile page that was turning all her icons upside down—without her asking. Although it was beginning to bother her that he never texted her back after her goofy I LOVE U dare.

"Wanna order dinner?" she asked, nudging Ned with her foot and picking up a phone so they could order from the hotel's room service menu.

"Huh?" said Ned, never taking his eyes off of the eighty-inch projector screen that dominated the room. Like A. A., Ned was tall and slim, but with a mess of curly blond hair inherited from his English dad.

"Forget it." A. A. shrugged. She knew better than to bother him when Resident Evil was on. "I'm not hungry, anyway. I'm still full from that tea."

"Uh-huh." Her brother nodded, cramming a hand into an enormous tub of popcorn on the couch and scattering kernels everywhere.

A. A. walked into her room. It was the smallest one in the suite—probably the former maid's closet—but she liked its coziness. Her mother had recently redecorated again, and instead of her princess bed with the canopies, she had a loft platform bed with a fluffy rug. She kind of missed the tufted headboard where she used to line up all her stuffed animals. Her mother's decorator had banished her collection into an opaque white lacquered trunk.

She threw her bag down on the bed, and only when she had closed the door firmly behind her did she check her phone for messages.

Sure, she had acted like texting laxjock that she loved him didn't mean anything, but she had to admit, she was worried. What if he thought she was serious? But then again, what if he thought she wasn't?

She fired up her computer and checked to see if he was online. Nope. He hadn't been online since that morning. Should she leave him a new comment? She mulled her options while her screen pinged with IMs from girls from class—everyone wanting to know more about Lauren's porky plastic surgery—when there was a sharp knock on the door.

"It's open," A. A. called.

A boy walked into the room. It was the same boy who'd suffered a good-natured defeat at her hands a few minutes earlier. He was dark-haired and handsome, with clear blue eyes and deep dimpled cheeks. Robert Austin Fitzpatrick the Third, or Tri, was hands down the cutest boy in the seventh grade at Gregory Hall. Alas, he was also the shortest boy in the seventh grade at Gregory Hall. He barely came up to A. A.'s chin. But then, so did most boys her age.

Tri's family owned the Fairmont Hotel, and the two of them had known each other since they were small enough to hide in the grandfather clocks in the grand ballroom. Growing up, they had learned to ride bikes up and down the hall corridors. His older brother was a friend of Ned's, and the two were familiar combatants during mutant zombie killfests.

"We're getting a pizza, do you want some?" he asked, taking a seat on the ornate bench in front of her bed. "Wow. Zebra stripes," he said, admiring the rug.

"I know. I can't stop her," A. A. said, sighing. Her mother's whirlwind interior design projects were a common annoyance. One year Jeanine had hired a feng shui master to realign the furniture, and he'd placed mammoth vases near all the doorways so that she banged her knee on one every time she left the room. "What kind of pizza?"

"Dunno. What kind do you want?" he asked. "Ned said you had the menu."

"Yeah, I think it's around here somewhere," said A. A., motioning to her messy desk.

"How was the tea?" he asked. Tri's older sisters were all Miss Gamble's girls and he was familiar with the school's social calendar.

"Okay." A. A. told him about the upchuck-inducing fountain and he laughed, but not in a mean way. Tri liked a good prank.

Her phone buzzed with a text message, vibrating against the wooden surface of her rolltop desk, and she grabbed it before it could fall off the edge. "Could you excuse me?" she asked, glancing down at her phone.

"Oh," Tri said, looking a little confused. "You want me to—okay. Sure."

"No—I—you can stay," she said, tapping her phone screen to see who had texted her. Her heart beat. She had wanted to read the message in private, but it was just Tri. They were like brother and sister. But she felt shy talking about her feelings for laxjock with him. Conversation with Tri always revolved around the discrepancies between the first and second Star Wars trilogies, whether there was life on other planets (Tri pro and A. A. con), and things you could explode in a microwave (marshmallows, bars of soap, CDs, but not the family cat).

She hit the message icon.

WANNA WTCH IDOL ON TVO 2GETHR W ME N LI?

It was just Ashley. A. A. exhaled, deflated. She tapped a quick message telling Ashley she was busy and they could Three-vo later.

"Waiting to hear from someone?" asked Tri, still poking around her desk and rummaging through her books and papers looking for the pizzeria menu.

"Huh? No." A. A. shook her head. "Don't touch that!" she said suddenly, slapping his hand away from her pink journal. She looked at the clock. It had been three hours since she'd sent laxjock her sappy text. Ugh. She had to do something. She scrolled down the list till she found his number and began tapping out a new text.

"Mushroom and sausage okay?" he asked, holding up the red and white menu.

A. A. nodded, without looking up. I WZ ONLY KDING! she wrote, and pressed the send button just as Tri got up to leave, closing the door behind him. She put down her phone and sighed. Maybe he thought she was being too forward. Maybe he never wanted to hear from her again.

But a few minutes later her phone buzzed back to life again.

She yelped when she saw the screen.

It was from him!

BUT I ♥ U 2 XOXOXOX

She pressed the phone close to her chest and smiled a small, secret smile. He was definitely amazing!

11

THAT H&M JACKET ISN'T THE
ONLY KNOCKOFF IN THE ROOM

"WHAT IS *SHE* DOING HERE?"
Ashley hissed, glaring at Lauren,
who had taken a seat at the round
table. "This meeting is for committee members only," she
said as she removed her new H&M jacket.

It was a copy of a much more expensive Stella McCartney
jacket, but she hoped no one would notice. The other day
her mother had flipped when she saw the latest bills from
Saks and had taken away Ashley's courtesy card, lecturing her
that twelve-year-olds did not need to carry two-thousand-
dollar handbags, blah blah blah, rampant materialism, blah
blah blah, excessive consumption, blah blah and blah. This
from a woman who spent a fortune on her skin-care regimen
alone. She said that Ashley was abusing her signing privileges

and told her she was lucky she wasn't taking away the handbag itself. With only her allowance to spend, Ashley was forced to downgrade labels. But she refused to downgrade her trend-setting Ashley Spencer style. People looked to her for their fashion cues. Hello.

"Relax, Ash. It's an after-school activity, anyone can sign up, remember?" A. A. said mildly as she stretched her legs on the seat in front of her and yawned widely without covering her mouth.

Ashley frowned. A. A. could be such a tomboy sometimes. It wasn't good for the Ashleys' enviable reputations if A. A. would persist in slouching down and acting like a boy. But it wasn't so much A. A.'s posture that was bothering her as what A. A. had said.

Technically, A. A. was right: *Technically*, anyone could sign up for any of the myriad after-school activities offered at Miss Gamble's, although Ashley couldn't imagine who'd want to waste their time at such boring activities as chorus, which was populated by off-key aspiring *Idol* wannabes, or theater, where you had to battle the budding drama queens who couldn't talk without "emoting" or walk without "expressing."

Even worse, who wanted to hang with the nerdy worker bees who ran yearbook and *The Gambler* (the school newspaper: three pages stapled together and released once a semester)? Then there was the lowest of the low—School Spirit, which was populated by doughy-faced girls who organized weekly bake sales and created handmade posters for pep rallies and field hockey games, and Fashion Club, which was started by two weirdos who wore bizarre outfits on free-dress days. The Ashleys would never be caught dead in something as trite as Fashion Club.

No. There was only one after-school activity worth signing up for, and everyone knew it. And that was Social Club, the club that ran the most important activity of all: the monthly mixers with the boys from Gregory Hall.

School had been in session for almost two weeks, and even Ashley was tired of making piggy noises whenever she saw Lauren. She had to give the girl credit. Even when someone drew a pig on her locker, Lauren never even looked upset. She walked the hallways with her nose in the air and looked straight ahead, never giving any sign that the teasing bothered her.

Still, the girl should know better than to crash a Social Club meeting. Everyone knew it was staffed by Ashleys and their SOAs only.

Ashley rapped on the podium and called the meeting to order. "Okay. So you all know what we have to do. Plan the best boy-girl dance *ever*." She wrote "Best Dance Ever" with four exclamation points on the whiteboard behind her.

"Yeah, and how are we going to do that if the dance starts at four p.m.?" asked Emma Rodgers, the way-too-opinionated leader of the popular eighth graders, who were all seated on the window ledges at the far side of the room. The eighth graders were too busy plotting how to crash high school parties to care about the mixer.

School policy dictated that all mixers and dances be held on school grounds from four to six in the afternoon. Every year the seventh and eighth graders campaigned for a later time—six to eight, seven to nine—and every year they were shot down.

Ashley reddened. "There's nothing we can do about that. I already asked."

"You know this means we have to change in the locker rooms," Montgomery Cunningham grumbled.

"We should just wear our uniforms," joked A. A. Ashley frowned. A. A. would probably do just that if she weren't an Ashley. She didn't seem to care what she wore, since everything ended up looking good on her. One time Ashley and Lili had noticed A. A. wearing odd-looking shorts to gym class, and they turned out to be her brother's boxer shorts. They were beyond horrified, but A. A. had merely shrugged.

"Dances are for losers," Eva Tobin, another eighth grader, declared.

"Shut up! The dance is going to be fun!" Ashley said, trying to restore order as the committee meeting began to degenerate into gossiping cliques. Sure, they could complain and moan forever about how an afternoon dance was strictly kid stuff. But they had to face facts. They went to an all-girls school. They had to take what they could get. Even if the dance was at a mega-lame hour, it still meant they could hang out with capital-B Boys.

Ashley put her hands on her hips and cleared her throat. "Okay. So what's our theme?"

"What about the sixties?" chirped Melody Myers, who could always be counted on to contribute, since she was a perennial hand-raiser. "I just saw *Grease*, and it was so cute. We could all wear poodle skirts and bobby socks—whatever those are."

"Cute! But isn't that the fifties?" A. A. asked, looking up from her phone.

"Fifties, sixties, what's the difference?" Melody asked.

"What about a Hawaiian theme?" Melody's friend Olivia DeBartolo suggested. "That could be cute, right? We could all dress in cute beachy clothes."

"Pass," Ashley said, crinkling her nose. "Do you guys really want to wear grass skirts and coconut boobs?"

"We could do an eighties theme," Lili suggested, sitting up straight in her chair. "Play a lot of Madonna, Prince, Billy Joel. Leggings are in now, and my mom said they were huge in the eighties, too. We could wear headbands and fingerless gloves and leg warmers! Ooh, leg warmers!"

"Eh," Ashley sniffed. She looked around the room to gauge interest level. A. A. was madly texting on her phone as usual, the eighth graders were completely ignoring her, and she knew the rest of the club would be happy to just let her decide.

"And we could rent, like, Pac-Man video games and Donkey Kong for the guys," said Lili, getting more and more enthusiastic.

"Sure, so they can totally ignore us at the dance," A. A. piped up, finally putting her phone away.

"Yeah, Lil, be serious. I'm so tired of eighties nostalgia, it's so cliché," Ashley finally declared.

"Well what are your ideas, then?" Lili asked, looking hurt and annoyed.

Ashley listened as the club discussed the merits of a winter wonderland theme. But the whole idea was nixed when A. A. pointed out that it was still autumn. There was a long, semi-heated debate on whether or not to serve food (would anyone actually eat in front of the boys?), and it looked like the meeting would accomplish exactly nothing, until a clear voice spoke from the back of the room.

"What about doing it like a celebrity event? We could do a red carpet—or a green one for Miss Gamble's. And the yearbook people can pose as paparazzi. And we could all get really, really dressed up," Lauren said, blushing deeply when all eyes turned to her.

Ashley raised an eyebrow. Okay, so it was not such a bad idea, but she couldn't very well acknowledge that.

"That doesn't sound too bad," Lili chimed in. "Don't you think, Ash?"

In response, Ashley flipped her hair over her shoulders and pointedly ignored Lili's comment. "I know," she announced, snapping her fingers. "We'll throw a VIP. A Very Important Party. We'll call it Miss Gamble's Goes Hollywood and have a velvet rope and lists and we could dress up in really cool clothes and get our pictures taken for the school newspaper."

Ashley watched as Lauren's color deepened. It was so obvious Ashley had just stolen her idea, but nobody seemed to care or notice. Lauren put her head down, her cheeks aflame. But she didn't say anything.

Just the way Ashley knew it would happen.

12

THE ENEMY OF YOUR ENEMY IS
YOUR . . . FRENEMY?

AFTER THE MEETING ENDED, LILI WATCHED as Lauren collected her things slowly so it wouldn't be so obvious that she had to walk out of the room by herself while everyone else was bunched into chattering groups. Why had she spoken up in favor of Lauren's idea? Especially since Ashley had declared Lauren a no-friend zone? If Lili stepped out of line . . . Well. What would happen? An idea began to form in her head.

Lili checked to see if Ashley had left the room, and when she was sure Ashley wouldn't see her, she ran up to Lauren. "Hey, wait up."

Lauren turned around. Her face was still bright red, from anger or embarrassment, Lili didn't know. She gave

Lauren the once-over. Lauren was wearing her hair back in a long, dark ponytail, and she'd lost the thick socks for a pair of cable-knit burgundy tights. Her uniform, Lili couldn't help but notice, was custom-tailored so it fit her perfectly. She made the green plaid kilt look almost chic. No wonder Ashley hated her.

"What?" asked Lauren, when Lili didn't say anything for a long moment.

"Gum?" Lili offered, holding out a Trident pack, not knowing quite how to start or what to say. The room where the meeting was held was one of the Gamble mansion's old bedrooms, with floral wallpaper and a brass chandelier hanging from the ceiling. An eighth grader stuck her head in the room looking for a forgotten binder and gave the two girls a curious look.

Lauren waited until she left before shaking her head. "No, thanks."

Lili shrugged and popped her gum. You weren't supposed to chew gum at Miss Gamble's. You also weren't supposed to slouch when you stood, sit with your legs spread, or talk loudly. But Lili was getting tired of playing by everyone else's rules.

"Listen . . . I know I'm probably not one of your favorite people right now," Lili said cautiously. "But I'd really like to talk to you."

Lauren snorted. "Why? So you can take credit for something I came up with, like your friend just did back there?" she asked, a cold edge to her voice.

"Look, I know what you're trying to do," Lili said softly. Why was she doing this? She looked at the swinging door. Her friends would be waiting for her, hiding behind a bus stop that had a perfect view of Gregory Hall across the street. They would be wondering where she was. Why was she wasting her time with Lauren? But something was compelling her to do it.

"What? What am I trying to do?" asked Lauren, blushing and twirling a lock of hair between her fingers.

"Get in with us," Lili said evenly.

Lauren gave her an eye roll and a dismissive snort. "Please."

"Fine." Lili slapped her notebook closed with a bang, as if considering the matter closed. "I thought I would try to help, but I guess you don't need any."

She'd approached Lauren on impulse, because she was mad at Ashley for being so rude to her at the meeting. But maybe it had been a mistake, after all. Lili began to walk away briskly. Maybe if she hurried, Ashley and A. A. wouldn't even notice that she had lagged behind.

"Wait."

Lili turned around slowly.

"I want to know what you wanted to say to me," Lauren said, biting her lip but looking Lili straight in the eye.

Lili took the gum out of her mouth and spit it gracefully into a Kleenex. "Well, I was going to tell you that Ashley doesn't like to make new friends. . . ."

"I don't need you to tell me that," said Lauren.

"Will you listen?" Lili asked. She couldn't tell who was more annoying, Ashley or Lauren—they kind of reminded her of each other.

"Go on," Lauren said stubbornly.

"Ashley doesn't like new people, but if you can give her something that she wants, then she'd be okay with having you around."

"Why are you telling me this?" Lauren asked.

Lili sighed. It was a question she was asking herself as well. Why rock the boat? Why befriend Lauren? She thought about how Ashley always got the red bag, the best seat, the ability to use her own name.

Ashley always got what she wanted, and she wanted Lauren "out." But maybe things would be more fun if Lauren was "in." Her mother's words rang in her ear. *You have to be your own person. Get out of Ashley's shadow.*

"I don't know," Lili said finally. "Maybe I'm just bored."

13

SOMETIMES IT'S NOT REALLY ABOUT THE BOY, BUT THE COMPANY

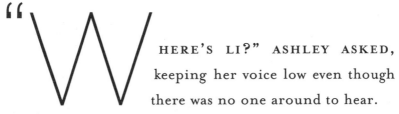

"WHERE'S LI?" ASHLEY ASKED, keeping her voice low even though there was no one around to hear.

"Dunno," A. A. whispered back. The two of them were being as quiet as possible, and every few seconds one of them would peek out from their hiding spot behind the bus shelter, eyes trained on the massive oak doors of Gregory Hall across the street.

The boys' school was located just a few blocks away from Miss Gamble's, housed in four interconnected ivy-covered brick buildings. Ashley watched several cars idling by the sidewalk as moms and drivers awaited their passengers. A crossing guard (a parent in an orange tech vest) stood at the corner, ready to marshal little ones to safety. The girls had been standing there for what seemed like hours, although in reality it was only a few minutes.

"Here I am," Lili said, materializing suddenly and squeezing in next to them. "I was in the bathroom," she explained. "Had to change my tampon," she added smugly. Lili always had to rub it in that she and A. A. had gotten theirs while Ashley was still waiting for hers.

"TMI!" Ashley gagged. Let A. A. and Lili bond over getting their "little friend," as her mom called it. Gross! She could wait forever if she had to. Who wanted to walk around with all those icky things between your legs? Ashley noticed that Lili had also put on an extra coat of lip gloss so that her lips were pink and shiny, and she'd gone a little heavy on the perfume. Ashley immediately checked her reflection in the glass and noticed A. A. was doing the same.

"Did I miss anything?" asked Lili, chancing a look from behind the glass wall with the STD poster urging young girls to get vaccinated.

"Nothing. But I think they just let out, I just heard the bell," replied Ashley, removing a tiny bottle of Benetint from her pocket and rubbing a little red stain on her cheeks, while A. A. pulled out her pigtails and shook out her hair.

"Has He come out yet?" Lili asked. They always spoke of Him in Capital Letters. He was that Important.

"No," Ashley said. "That's why we're waiting, duh!" She wrinkled her nose and sniffed the air. "Lil, what did you put on?"

"Why?" Lili asked. "It's YSL. I nicked it from my mom's dresser." She stuck her wrist directly under Ashley's nose. "Doesn't it smell good?"

"Um, yeah," Ashley replied.

"Whatever it is, I think I'm allergic," said A. A., coughing into her hand.

"You're a spaz!" Lili exclaimed, pushing her backward, and A. A. pushed back, the two of them giggling.

"Stop it! He'll see us!" Ashley ordered, shushing them, and the two girls calmed down. Serious business was at hand. She staked her place in the very front, with a direct view to the sidewalk across the street.

"Oh, look—there—there he is," A. A. said excitedly as the doors suddenly opened and a stream of boys in blue blazers exited in a mad rush, spilling out into the street. "I see him!" She peered out from behind the bus shelter, accidentally surprising an elderly woman who was waiting for the bus. A. A. ducked her head back behind the glass to give her two friends room to take a look.

Lili stood on her tiptoes. "Ash, could you move? You're hogging the prime spot, as usual," she complained.

"Am not!" Ashley protested. Lili always said that, and

nothing could be further from the truth. She could barely see the top of his head.

"SHUSH!" A. A. warned.

"God . . ." Ashley sighed, reflexively putting her hands over her heart.

"He's just *sooo* . . . ," Lili cooed.

"Cute," finished A. A., pushing her two friends to the side so she could get a shot with her cell phone camera.

Cute wasn't even the word, Ashley thought. More like Perfect. Or Unbelievable. The object of their affection was a tall, towheaded boy. Like the other boys, he wore a navy blazer, a white shirt with a blue and gold tie, and gray flannel pants. But even from a distance, he stood out from the crowd. His hair was a shining crown of gold ringlets, he had the broad shoulders and slim hips of a swimmer or a tennis player, and he walked with a confident, loping stride.

There was something nonchalant and easy about him. Ashley even loved the way he wore his clothes—the blazer was pushed up to his elbows, his gray flannel pants were worn too long so the cuffs dragged on the ground, and his tie was askew. A lacrosse stick was slung behind him with his backpack. He walked across the street, maddeningly close to the bus station, then turned the corner and disappeared down the hill.

"Okay, he won't see us now. Let's go," Ashley said, inching

out from their hiding place once she was confident they would not be discovered. The other two followed after her, and they walked in the same direction he had gone.

"Look," said A. A., showing them the fuzzy, pixilated image she had taken. "I'm so making this my screen saver."

"A. A., can you please get a new phone? I can barely see him in this," Lili complained, returning it.

"Do you really think he has a girlfriend?" Ashley asked, keeping an eye on him from two blocks away. The boy stopped by a Starbucks for his daily double-shot espresso. She'd ordered it once after watching him down one and was totally disgusted. She couldn't believe he could drink something so foul.

"That's what I heard," A. A. said. A. A.'s brother knew him from school, so she always had the best information.

"I can't believe he's taken," Lili lamented.

"I know." Ashley sighed. The boy's name was William Augustus Reddy, Billy for short. The three of them had been crushing on him forever, and at the moment, Ashley was content to share him with her friends, like a bag of no-salt, fat-free soy crisps. But make no mistake, he was meant to be hers and hers alone.

Like her, Billy Reddy was from one of the wealthiest and most prominent families in the Bay Area. His family had founded the Reddy Oil Company and lived in the Reddy

Chateau, an imposing, fifty-thousand-square-foot structure in Pacific Heights that was so big that Mrs. Reddy had started a private Montessori school on the first floor for her grandchildren, according to Ashley's mom. The family was also famous for owning a fleet of private jets that were always at the "Reddy."

On some days Ashley was almost positive that he noticed her walking behind him and would catch her eye with a smile. She watched as he left the Starbucks, and after a few minutes, she resumed her shadowing, followed closely by her two friends. Most days Billy walked directly home from school after his coffee fix, although sometimes, like today, he stopped by a couple of the stores on Fillmore Street, browsing in the bookstore or record shop for CDs.

While Billy was in the tiny storefront of the record shop, Ashley suggested to the others that they stop by a nearby deli to load up on snacks. Surveillance always made her hungry. She brought her nonfat selections to the front cashier, where Lili was paying for three Diet Cokes and A. A. waited with her choice from the candy aisle. They paid quickly.

"Pop Rocks?" offered A. A., tearing open the foil packet and shaking the tiny candies onto her hand as they walked out of the store.

Ashley shook her head. "You know, if you eat Pop Rocks

and Coke, you die," she warned, looking meaningfully at the Diet Coke in Lili's hand.

"That's not true, it's just an urban myth," Lili retorted, although Ashley noticed she made sure to swallow her soda before putting a wad of Pop Rocks into her mouth.

"Wish we could invite Billy to the dance," said Ashley, opening up a bag of unsalted popcorn and digging in.

"Oh, yeah. Come party with us from four to six." Lili nodded. "He'll be *really* into that." Sometimes Ashley wished Lili would let up a little. A girl could dream, couldn't she?

"Seventh-grade boys are so immature," said A. A., who'd told them earlier that she had no interest in the dance, especially since she was involved with someone who was older and way cooler. "I can't possibly fathom a relationship with a boy our age. What would we do? Play Monopoly?"

"But we'll still have fun," Ashley whined. She hated it when A. A. got all smug about her so-called boyfriend and acted like she was so beyond them all. It was only a few months ago that they had avidly spied on the seventh graders at the dance, wishing they were old enough to join. "Everyone can come to my house to get ready, since it's just across the street. Isn't the VIP thing genius?" she asked.

"Yeah. About that. You should really give Lauren a break sometimes," Lili said lightly.

"Why?" Ashley asked sourly. Hadn't Lili been there when they all decided Lauren was still a zero? Hadn't Lili been the one who made up the pig-nose thing? "What's up with you? It's like you have a girl crush on her or something."

Lili flushed. "Whatever. Forget it."

Ashley was so busy being annoyed with Lili that she didn't notice that as they were walking, Billy had stopped at the crosswalk, and the three of them were now standing just a few feet behind him. "Omigod! He's turning around! He's looking! He'll see us!" she whispered frantically, fearing imminent exposure. She couldn't fathom anything worse than being discovered. It was almost like being caught with no clothes on.

"What are we going to do?" Lili panicked.

"Hide!" A. A. hissed.

"Over here! Follow me!" Ashley ordered, like a general leading the troops into battle, and dove into a nearby rosebush for protection. Lili and A. A. followed, laughing and pushing as they stumbled into one another in their haste to scramble for shelter.

"Omigod! I think I'm bleeding!"

"Whose idea was this?"

"Aah, I have a thorn in my side!"

"Will you guys please shut up?" Ashley pleaded, trying to keep her voice as low as possible. Her friends gave her such a headache sometimes. It was such a burden having to be the brains of the operation all the time.

"What's going on in there?" a male voice asked from the sidewalk.

The three of them screamed. Pop Rocks, popcorn, and Diet Coke spilled everywhere. Ashley peered out of the prickly foliage anxiously, convinced that their cover was totally blown.

But it wasn't Billy Reddy who stood in front of them—it was a very confused-looking Tri Fitzpatrick.

14

GUESSING GAMES

"WE'RE SAFE. IT'S JUST TRI," A. A. told the other girls. Trust Ashley to find the worst hiding place in the world. Who in their right mind jumps into a rosebush? Even worse, they'd lost the trail. There was no sign of Billy Reddy anywhere. A. A. didn't know whether to be relieved or disappointed as she picked her way out of the bushes onto the sidewalk to examine the tiny scratches on her arms and legs,

"Hi, Tri," Ashley and Lili chorused as they, too, pushed branches aside and climbed their way out of the disastrous hiding place. They smiled at Tri like they would smile at a pet dog. A. A. knew they didn't think you could really take a guy seriously when he was shorter than you, and as much as it pained A. A. to do so, she had to agree.

"Way to go, Ash, I think I'm scarred for life," Lili

complained, exaggerating as usual, since the cut she was talking about was barely even bleeding. "Does anyone have a Band-Aid?"

"Yeah, can you, like, find us a more comfortable hiding place next time?" asked A. A., shaking her head and showering rose petals all over the sidewalk.

"Emergency measures had to be taken," Ashley said. "I didn't hear either of you come up with anything else." Of course, she couldn't understand what the big deal was, since she had escaped the bushes relatively unscathed. Typical Ashley. The girl had a good-luck charm over her head.

Tri regarded them with an I'll-never-understand-girls look on his handsome face. "What's up? What were you guys doing in there?"

"Nothing." Ashley giggled, brushing out a few leaves from her sweater. "We were just—"

Lili elbowed her. "Shhh."

"What's the big deal?" asked Tri, looking to A. A. for an explanation. But she merely shrugged, embarrassed to have been caught on their private expedition. Tri wouldn't understand—he'd think it was dumb, and it *was* dumb, but there were some things that only girls should know. At least until Ashley opened her big mouth and told him all about their "walk and stalk."

"A stalk and what?" Tri asked, his forehead crinkling

adorably, looking more confused than ever.

"Ash, shut up!" Lili yelped, clamping both hands over Ashley's mouth before her friend could elaborate further. "He *knows* him!" she warned, as if she were in a spy movie and Ashley were giving up the goods to the enemy.

"What's the big deal?" asked Ashley, giving Lili a hard pinch. "What could it hurt? Tri's our buddy," she went on, giving Tri a big grin. "A walk and stalk. We follow Billy Reddy around after school. It's our extracurricular. Didn't A. A. tell you? I thought she told you everything," she smirked.

"What's the big deal with Billy Reddy?" Tri asked, still looking flabbergasted by the three squealing girls covered with a combination of candy, popcorn, and greenery. He looked to A. A. for help, but she refused to meet his eye.

"We're in love. All three of us," Ashley singsonged.

"With Billy?" Tri asked, still stubbornly on topic. The way he said it was as if they had declared undying affection for some cheesy boy-band clone. A. A. cringed—he'd never let her hear the end of it when they hung out later. She could just hear his voice now: *A. A.'s in love with Billy Reddy, A. A.'s in love with Billy Reddy. . . .* She would have to shut him up by killing off all his zombies in record time and showing no mercy.

"Yes, with Billy. But you can't tell him, okay?" Lili said bossily. "Don't ruin it for us." She wagged a finger in his face.

"Do I still have leaves in my hair?" asked A. A., trying to change the subject. It was way too awkward talking about Billy with Tri. She wished they could talk about something else, but everyone ignored her.

Ashley grinned wickedly. "A. A. is convinced her secret online boyfriend is Billy Reddy."

That was a low blow. She looked at Ashley, horrified. "That was a secret!" she cried, punching her on the arm. The afternoon after the tea, she had told Ashley the truth about laxjock in a fit of female bonding. Obviously that had been a terrible idea. Ashley could no more keep a secret than shop for things on sale.

"Oh. Oops," Ashley said. "Ow!" She massaged her forearm where A. A. had struck her. "That hurt!"

"What secret online boyfriend?" asked Tri, looking keener than ever. A. A. thought his eyes looked like they would bug out of his skull. What, was she not allowed to have secrets of her own? Tri really needed to get a life.

"Yeah, what secret online boyfriend? I thought he was a real guy. You mean you've never met?" Lili asked, her eyes narrowing. *Now you've done it*, A. A. thought. Lili hated being left out of the loop and would make her pay dearly for keeping secrets from her—especially secrets that Ashley knew.

"What's this, Guantanamo?" A. A. huffed. She could feel herself turning bright red and tried to look bored and indifferent. *Of course* she didn't really believe Billy Reddy was laxjock. But if she was completely honest with herself, she secretly hoped he would turn out to be her guy. After all, these were the facts. Fact Number One: His online handle was "laxjock." And who was the best lacrosse player at Gregory Hall? Billy Reddy, who'd been on the varsity team ever since his freshman year. Fact Number Two: Laxjock went to a private school. Billy Reddy went to Gregory Hall— *a private school*. Fact Number Three: Laxjock lived in San Francisco. And so did Billy Reddy! Case closed.

The other night she and laxjock had spent the entire evening IMing each other. He was so easy to talk to, and they talked about everything—how she missed her mom when she went on her crazy adventures around the globe, how she never really talked to her dad since her parents' divorce, how she was worried she was going to fail math and get kicked out of Miss Gamble's, how she loved her friends but sometimes wished they would drop dead.

Now Ashley had blabbed her most cherished secret to the world, and Tri was watching her with a strange look on his face. She knew he thought of her merely as this gangly tomboy he'd been friends with forever, and she wished he would stop looking at her that way. Just because she had a secret online boyfriend didn't mean they had to stop hanging out.

"Anyway, it's no big deal. Yes, I have a boyfriend. No, we

haven't met yet, but that doesn't mean anything. We're going to meet, really soon," she said a bit defensively. Last night she and laxjock had confessed to each other that they were scared to meet, since their relationship was already so "perfect" online.

Tri put his earbuds back in. "All right. Whatever. I'll see you guys later," he said, already dialing up a song on his iPod.

"Hold on," Ashley said, playfully pulling out his earphones. "You coming to our dance next month?"

He cocked an eyebrow. "Miss Gamble's Afternoon Delight?"

"Shut up. It's not our fault our school is overprotective," retorted Ashley.

"Yeah. I'll be there." He nodded.

"Make sure you get all your friends to come too, 'kay?" Lili asked. Good call for Lil. Having more girls than boys at the mixer was a traumatic and not-unheard-of event at Miss Gamble's.

"See you, Tri," A. A. called, and he saluted her as he walked away. Ashley and Lili wanted to window-shop the boutiques on Union Street, but she didn't feel like hanging out anymore and went straight back to the penthouse.

Tri came over later that night with a bunch of other guys to watch some gorefest on cable. Surprisingly, he didn't mention anything about what had happened that afternoon, and

A. A. didn't bring it up either. They were content to watch college kids get carved up by psychos on vacation. When the movie ended, Tri and his brother went home and A. A. logged in online.

She called up laxjock's home page and sent him a message. Lili was right. It was ridiculous that she didn't even know who he was or what he looked like. Did she really have a boyfriend? Or was it just some phantom dude with an IP connection? It was time to face reality. She typed two words onscreen and sent them whizzing to his in-box.

"Let's meet."

15

A CUTE BOY MAKES THE BEST PUH (PERSONAL UMBRELLA HOLDER)

"SOMETHING BOTHERING YOU?" DEX asked, when Lauren climbed into the Bentley the next morning.

"No, why?" she replied, shaking her head.

"You've been quiet lately," Dex said, cocking his head and studying her before getting into the front seat. "Those girls being mean to you again?"

"I'd rather not talk about it," Lauren snapped. When she found out the Ashleys had spread that ridiculous rumor about her family being "connected," she got so mad she really did feel like "whacking" somebody. Her dad had worked really, really hard for his success. The Mafia thing was so off base it wasn't even worth getting upset about, but she couldn't help herself.

And the story about her nose being sculpted from a pig's butt—well, that was just too absurd to even pay attention to. They were just jealous, she kept telling herself. Living well was the best revenge, her dad always said, but what was the point of living large when there was no one to see it? If a Gucci bag was bought at the outlet and no one saw, would it count?

But Dex wouldn't quit. "Your mom said—"

"I know what my mom said. Can we just—"

"Okay. Fine. I'll drop it. But riddle me this, Batgirl. Why do girls from your school keep asking me if I'm from New Jersey and then giggling and running off?" he asked as he backed out of the steep driveway, zigzagging expertly so that the car didn't brush up against the newly installed solar-powered entry lights.

"Just drive," Lauren ordered. It had been a few days since Ashley Li—the cute Chinese one who always looked so tiny and perfect—had offered her that unsolicited advice about dealing with Ashley Spencer, and Lauren still didn't know what to make of it. All night Lauren had tossed and turned, wondering what she could offer the Queen of the Mean. She couldn't think of anything.

Ashley Spencer was a golden girl. She had everything a twelve-year-old girl could ever possibly want. Looks. Clothes. Money. Cool friends. What could Lauren offer her that she didn't have already? Nothing. Absolutely nothing. It was so frustrating. What was the point of looking like an

Ashley from the outside if she was still dorky Lauren on the inside? She had to become one of the Ashleys somehow. She had to infiltrate that tight-knit group in order to destroy it. Corruption always started from within. Just like the fall of the Roman Empire. And history was her favorite subject.

As Lauren brooded on her predicament, a song by her favorite new hot-girl band, the StripHall Queens, came on the radio. Dex turned up the music, which she appreciated, since he'd told her more than once that he didn't know how she could stand to listen to that "hooker anthem."

She should treat him better, she thought. Dex was a good guy. She'd known him since she was little, and over the summer, she and Dex had really gotten close. Her parents were always too busy with the business, and her older sister had moved to L.A. for college, so Dex was practically the only family she had.

"Hey, so what's going on with you and your new girl?" she asked. Dex always had a new girlfriend; it was like a revolving door every week. She could never keep up with all their names. He'd gone through a cheerleader phase, a rich-bitch phase, then a number of flighty New Age types who were always offering to forecast her horoscope.

"Who said I had a new girl?" He laughed, turning the wheel and zooming ahead of a Porsche that had cut him off at the last corner.

"Don't you always?" Lauren teased.

"Maybe," said Dex, rolling down the car window and letting some fresh air inside. Lauren noticed a blush creeping up his ears.

"Why so mysterious?" she asked. Dex always opened up about his retinue of chicks. She'd learned to be skeptical of boys since knowing Dex. He was always giving her dating advice, which was especially sweet since he never seemed to notice that Lauren didn't date. She appreciated his interest, however. It made her feel better that Dex believed that someday soon her phone would start ringing off the hook, with boys lined up to take her out. So far, though, it hadn't happened.

"Why so curious?" he shot back.

Lauren shrugged. She was just making small talk to take the heat off her own problems. Although she did like to hear about Dex's love life since it was far more interesting than her own. She knew her mom quizzed Dex on her life behind her back. Was Lauren happy? Did she have any friends? Her mother had allowed her to get the makeover only to stop the teasing. Her parents threatened to pull her out of school entirely if things didn't change, but Lauren couldn't let that happen.

Miss Gamble's was the best primary school in the city. If she didn't graduate from Miss Gamble's, she'd never get into Exeter, her dream prep school, and if she didn't go to Exeter, she'd never get into Harvard, her dream college, and if she didn't go to Harvard, she'd never be able to launch a career as the next Oprah. Lauren had big dreams for her future. It was the only thing that kept her present tolerable.

"Shallow dating pool?" she teased Dex.

"Nah, I got a lady friend, but I'm taking it slow this time, you know?" Dex shrugged.

Lauren nodded. She settled back into the seat. Outside it began to rain. Big fat droplets drummed on the roof of the car, and she was glad she had brought her bright red slicker that day. Dex drove the car slowly, then pulled to the curb without warning and threw the passenger-side door open.

"Hey, Billy! Get in," he called, waving to a tall, drenched youth making his way up the hilly sidewalk.

"What are you doing?" asked Lauren, a little alarmed.

"Giving my boy a ride," Dex told her, as a very good-looking blond boy, his hair wet and plastered to his face, clambered into the front seat. "You don't mind, do you?" added Dex. "We got a big game against Saint A's this week-end, can't have my star forward coming down with the flu."

Lauren shook her head. Especially when she saw who the hitchhiker was. It was the same boy she'd seen the Ashleys tailing the other afternoon. She had spotted the trio walking slowly behind him the other day and had watched with amusement as the wicked threesome dove into some bushes when he turned around.

"Hey, I'm Billy Reddy," the boy said, turning around and

flashing Lauren a heart-melting smile.

"I know," Lauren answered. It was charming how he acted like he was just a normal kid walking to school and not some sort of celebrity. The Reddys were the most talked-about family in San Francisco. There were whole websites devoted to their genealogy and scandals. Lauren knew all about his older brother, a Hollywood movie star who had a baby with a former prostitute; his sister, the heroin junkie, who'd just been packed off to rehab; and his other sister, whose five-star million-dollar wedding to an Arabian sheik was in the pages of all the society magazines.

"Really? I don't think we've met," Billy said, a dimple winking on each cheek.

"That's Lauren," said Dex, fiddling with the radio and trying to find a better station. Lauren figured he didn't want to be caught by Billy listening to sluttybop.

"Oh, yeah. Dex told me about you. Your dad's Sergei Page, right?"

Lauren nodded. Dex talked to Billy Reddy about her? Billy Reddy knew who she was?

"I love YourTV. I put up stuff all the time," said Billy, still turned around so that he could talk to her directly. "Hey, Dex, did you get someone to work the camera for the game this weekend?"

"Oh, yeah. We're all set." Dex nodded.

"You should come watch a game sometime," Billy told her. "We never have enough of a crowd. And Dex is a great coach. Kicks our asses most of the time, but I guess we deserve it. This weekend's an away game, but maybe next week you could come down."

"Sure," Lauren said casually. Had Billy Reddy just invited her to watch his lacrosse game? She had to pinch herself to make sure she was awake. He was probably just being friendly, trying to get one more body into the stands. You'd think the lacrosse games would be packed. But now that she thought about it, they played down at the marina, where the winds were brutal, and Dex had told her that almost no one came to watch the games except for the players' parents.

"Cool." Billy winked.

The car pulled up to the school, and Lauren noticed that Ashley Spencer was climbing out of a tan Range Rover right behind them. She suddenly remembered Ashley Li's words. *If you can give her something she wants, she'd be okay with having you around.* Lauren looked at the front seat of her car and knew the answer.

"Dex—I can't seem to get this door open," she complained, keeping an eye on Ashley, who was kissing her dad good-bye.

"Huh?"

Lauren pretended to fumble with the handle. "Yeah, Daddy said there was something wrong with it the other day."

"There's something wrong with my baby?" Dex asked, stricken. He treated the Bentley like a favored child. When he wasn't driving it, Lauren saw him waxing the finish or lovingly detailing the wheels.

"I'll get it," offered Billy, getting out of his seat just as Lauren had hoped he would.

Lauren also hoped that Ashley would notice as Billy held the door open for her patiently, but Ashley was fumbling in her bag for her cell phone. Lauren would have to make the moment last just a little longer. "Could you hold this?" she asked, handing him her dad's golf umbrella, which she'd found in the backseat. "I hate getting my hair wet."

"Sure," Billy said, taking the umbrella and dutifully holding it open for her. Lauren peered from the corner of her eye. Ashley was now chatting on the phone, probably to her two other stuck-up friends, so Lauren took her time climbing out of the car, locking her knees together, then sliding out of the seat gracefully. She took the umbrella from Billy and gave him a quick hug, pressing her smooth cheek against his damp one.

"*Grazie.*"

"Anytime," he said amiably.

Lauren chanced a look in Ashley's direction, but the arctic blonde had already disappeared through the school doors. Had Ashley seen them together? She could only hope.

16

A CHANGE OF HEART OR MERELY A CHANGE OF TUNE?

HAT DID NOT JUST HAPPEN, ASHLEY THOUGHT. She did *not* just see Billy Reddy with Lauren Page. It was completely insane. Billy was saving himself for *her.* How the hell did Lauren even know the guy? She tore her eyes away from the two of them hugging and stomped into school in a black mood, heading straight for the lockers without even greeting her two friends with her usual verve. Ashley folded up her umbrella so violently that a shower of raindrops splattered on A. A., who was gathering books for their next class.

"Okay, who told you that shopping causes acne?" A. A. joked, when she saw the look on Ashley's face.

"Ha-ha," Ashley said mirthlessly, shoving the umbrella away. She slammed her locker door with a bang, taking satisfaction in rattling the hinges. "I just saw . . . ," she said, pausing to place an ouchless elastic between her teeth while she pulled her hair up into a high ponytail. She wasn't even sure if she could utter the words.

"Saw what?" A. A. prompted as they walked out of the new glassed-in annex, which housed the lockers, organic local foods refectory, and state-of-the-art music center, into the main building.

"Huh? Oh, nothing, forget it." Ashley shrugged, deciding against telling A. A. what she'd just witnessed. Before she jumped the gossip gun, there had to be some rational explanation for why the boy she loved was with the girl she loathed.

She was still annoyed when they arrived at their first class of the day: Manners & Morals, with Miss Charm. Now there was a teacher who was one slice short of a whole pizza. Miss Charm was the school's flighty but sweet etiquette teacher, another one of Miss Gamble's spinster alums who'd returned to serve on the faculty or administration out of the deep affection they felt for the place. Ashley had a hard time imagining the school's staff— myopic Miss Moos, eccentric Miss Charm, effusive Miss Murphy—outside of the sheltered, cozy society of the all-girls school. It was as if they were frozen in time and place.

The class was taught in a sunny room in the front of

the mansion, and when they arrived Ashley noticed that all the desks were pushed to the edges of the room in a semi-circle. Lili was already waiting for them and waved them over to the two seats she was saving. "Did the mirror say you weren't the prettiest?" she asked, upon seeing the dark expression on Ashley's face.

God. Her friends knew her too well. She never could hide her feelings from them. Ashley dredged up a smile, but her heart wasn't in it. Lauren Page and Billy Reddy—it just didn't make any sense. Especially when she, Ashley Spencer, had yet to even say one word to the guy? Hello.

But she couldn't dwell on it now, since class was starting, and etiquette was one of the few subjects she actually enjoyed and did well in. Not that being a C student bothered her in the least. She'd read in a glossy magazine she was flipping through at the salon once that the world was run by C students, and she fully expected to rule the world one day, regardless of her poor marks. As far as Ashley was concerned, they were a nonissue. After all, there was nothing average about her looks.

"Good morning, good morning," Miss Charm sang as she walked briskly into the room, her hair piled on top of her head in a beehive. "Girls, today we're going to go over the conduct for a very special event. Do you know what it is?" She clasped her hands in delight. Miss Charm was given to extravagant hand gestures. It was part of her, um, charm. "Your first ballroom dance!"

Ashley smirked at her friends, but she was not immune to the small, birdlike woman's enthusiasm for the project. The afternoon mixer, or the "VIP," as Social Club had dubbed it, was also supposed to be a ballroom dance. Not in a cheesy *Dancing with the Stars* fashion, of course—no way were Miss Gamble's girls going to don purple sequins and nude panty hose—but as a quasi-formal affair wherein young gentlemen and young ladies were introduced to the ways of polite society.

At least, that was the idea.

Speaking of the dance, major preparations were in order, and like a good leader, Ashley had delegated the entire task of putting on the production to Lili and A. A. Why stress about a million little things when you could get your friends to stress for you? Ashley tapped out a text to Lili's phone.

HOW IS MXR PLANNING GOING?

Her phone buzzed immediately with a reply.

ON IT. EVERYTHING GR8. DON'T WORRY.

Ashley looked up at Lili, who winked. Oh, well. If she said not to worry . . . and God knew Lili was an organization queen—the books in her locker were arranged in a sliding scale on the color spectrum and her binders were color-coded and indexed according to subject. Ashley slipped her phone back into the side pocket of her handbag just as Miss Charm walked over and placed a hand on her shoulder.

"I'm going to pretend to be a young man at the party," the teacher said. "Ashley, why don't you stand up, please. You will play the part of a young lady. I hope it's not too strenuous a role."

Ashley laughed because the rest of the class was laughing, even though she didn't find the joke funny, and obediently stood up in front of her desk while Miss Charm walked toward her from the opposite side of the room.

"I am a young man from Gregory Hall who has just entered the dance. Now I stop and see a girl I'd like to ask to dance. I walk over to where she is seated. And I bow in front of her," said Miss Charm, bowing like a man, bending at the waist with her right hand folded above her stomach. "Now, as the young lady who has been approached, what do you do?"

This was why Ashley loved Manners & Morals. If she had her way, all social interaction would entail people bowing to her. "I curtsy," she replied, making a small dip with her knees and holding her uniform skirt up.

"Good. A little less neck on the curtsy. Your whole body must go down, not just a tilt of the head. Try it again, dear."

Ashley tried it again with more knee and less neck.

"Very good. Excellent." Miss Charm beamed. Ashley beamed back. Who wanted to learn new math when old-fashioned etiquette was so much more fun?

Miss Charm regarded the class. "So now the boy turns to the girl and asks, 'May I have this dance?' And if you would like to dance with the young man, how do you respond?"

"Certainly, thank you," Ashley replied as they'd been taught. She smiled, picturing Billy Reddy crossing the room in a dark frock coat and gray trousers, a dashing Mr. Darcy to her Keira Knightley—er, Elizabeth Bennet. Then she remembered that Lauren Page had a better chance of playing Elizabeth than she did at the moment, and she frowned.

Miss Charm began to lead her in the box steps of the waltz, but Ashley had a question she wanted answered first. "But what if I don't want to dance with the boy?" she asked, her imagination conjuring up a pimply Mr. Collins type— like that freak who'd been obsessed with her since prekindergarten, Jonathan Tessin, with the sweat problem— shuffling over to her side.

The class tittered, and Ashley glowed. She absolutely adored being the center of attention.

"You must respond, 'Not right now, but thank you for asking,'" Miss Charm directed. "Etiquette is all about kindness, girls. That's why it's called polite society. One must never hurt anyone's feelings."

"But aren't you just leading him on, then?" asked A. A., without raising her hand.

"Yeah, can't you just say, 'Get lost, loser'?" Lili called with a grin.

"Heavens, no!" Miss Charm laughed. "You'll scare the poor boys away. I do hope that you girls agree to dance with every boy who is courageous enough to cross the room and ask for your hand."

Yeah, that was likely, Ashley thought as the twenty girls in class groaned, and there was grumbling and merriment all around.

"Now we shall practice," Miss Charm said, releasing her hold on Ashley and turning on the iPod player by the whiteboard. The soft sounds of Chopin's Waltz in C Sharp Minor filled the room.

Ashley ended up being partnered with A. A., while Lili had the unfortunate luck to dance with Sheridan Riley, who was sure to talk her ear off and ask a million questions about something inane like her socks and where she could get the same exact ones and exactly how far up the calf they should be pulled up, or in last year's case, scrunched down. Being the subject of Sheridan's obsession was flattering, but ultimately exhausting in its quest for detail.

Especially on the days when your socks were just . . . socks.

As they glided around the room, Ashley noticed Lauren dancing with Katie Tanaka, another of the class's bigmouth girls. Katie was sure to know the latest news. "Let's go over there," she said, pulling A. A. to that side of the room so she could overhear their conversation without appearing too obvious about it.

A. A. was doing her space-cadet bit, looking over Ashley's shoulder and going through the motions of the waltz's box steps, and didn't object to being directed. Ashley edged a little closer to where Katie and Lauren were pirouetting. Miss Charm was seated by the window bench, going over the syllabus for her next class, and didn't pay attention as most of the girls stopped waltzing and started talking instead. Ashley chided herself on having to stoop so low—gossip usually originated from her and the other Ashleys, not the other way around—but this was the matter of Billy Reddy. The love of her life. She inched forward a little more. They were so close to Lauren and Katie that she could have reached over and pulled Lauren's hair if she wanted to.

Jackpot. Katie was just saying his name. . . .

"So I heard Billy Reddy dropped you off at school this morning," Katie was saying. "What's the deal? Is he your boyfriend or something?"

Ashley almost tripped over A. A.'s high-heeled saddle

shoes in an effort to hear Lauren's reply. Billy had a new girlfriend—it couldn't be *Lauren*, could it? God wouldn't be that mean! Maybe God was pissed that she hadn't come through on her promise to be nicer to her parents. But then, God hadn't been able to get her mom to raise her allowance, so maybe they were even.

"Nah, we're just really good friends," she heard Lauren say. "He's an awesome guy. But I'm not his girlfriend. Is that what people are saying? How funny!"

Ashley breathed a sigh of relief. She jerked A. A. back toward the other end of the room with a smile.

"What the eff?" A. A. complained, coming out of her daze. "And why do you look so happy all of a sudden?"

"I just realized I have a gift card I still haven't spent at Saks," Ashley lied. "Now dip me." There was absolutely no chance in hell any of them would ever make use of anything they learned in class today at the dance. Unless you could waltz to gangsta rap. But it was still fun to practice.

Maybe Lili was right after all. Lili often was. Maybe Lauren wasn't *such* a zero as she had originally thought. Especially not if she was friends with Billy Reddy. Maybe she should give her a chance. After all, like Miss Charm said, etiquette was all about kindness. Ashley saw herself as a kind soul. She would *let* Lauren be her friend. Really, it was the least she could do for the poor girl.

17

THE PRIVATE JET SET

THE SAN RAFAEL AIRPORT WAS SO SMALL IT didn't even seem like it could technically be called an airport, consisting as it did of just two airstrip lanes and a minuscule terminal that housed the passenger waiting area. Flying private was certainly a different experience, Lili thought. There was no need to fight crowds, or to make sure all your liquids fit into three-ounce containers, or have to walk barefoot on a public floor through a metal detector. The atmosphere in the captain's lounge was clubby and relaxed, in stark contrast to the usual harried chaos at SFO. Private was definitely the *only* way to travel.

That morning a shiny black stretch limousine had picked her up first thing, and at the wheel was the slick, gorgeous guy she'd seen driving Lauren on the first day of school, who introduced himself as "Bond, Dex Bond."

When she climbed inside the car, Ashley and A. A. were already ensconced in the comfy backseat, drinking mocktails out of champagne flutes. They were dressed as she was, in oversize Christian Dior sunglasses with big, gold-plated *D*s on each side and black Couture Couture fur-lined trench coats—suitably warm for another freezing San Francisco day. The three of them agreed that the limo ride that took them across the Golden Gate Bridge to Marin County was a generous and extravagant gesture on Lauren's part, although Ashley had pronounced her virgin appletini "too sweet."

Last week Ashley had invited Lauren to join their table at lunch out of the blue, which had effectively turned the Ashleys into a foursome. Later Lili discovered that word had it Lauren was a "very close friend" of Billy Reddy's, which explained why Ashley had suddenly stopped playa-hating.

Lili had no idea how Lauren managed *that*—as far as Lili knew, Billy Reddy didn't waste his time on seventh graders. But whether or not it was true, it was a brilliant move on Lauren's part. It looked as if the girl was finally taking Lili's advice. Lauren promised to take them all to Billy Reddy's next lacrosse game, and the Ashleys couldn't wait. To seal the deal, Lauren told them she thought Billy was cute, for sure, but she didn't *like him* like him. Fair enough, since Billy was meant to be Lili's one true love, anyone could see that.

So Lauren was one of them . . . for the time being. And

Lili had been right about more than one thing: Having Lauren around had made life a little more interesting. She could certainly think of worse things in the world than taking a limo to a private jet bound for Los Angeles for a day of shopping and then back to San Francisco for a sleepover afterward.

Now she and her friends were at the airport, crowded around a circular bar in front of a picture window with a view of the grassy wetlands, their attention focused on Dex, who really was too cute for words, as he stood behind the counter, pouring rounds of energy drinks, telling jokes, and showing them card tricks.

"Ace of spades," he said, as he turned over A. A.'s card and showed her the black ace.

"How did you know?" A. A. marveled, turning to her friends and giggling.

"That's for me to know and you to find out," Dex teased, reshuffling cards like a pro.

It was obvious that A. A. thought Dex was adorable. She couldn't stop blushing whenever he looked at her. That girl was so boy-crazy she went gaga over every attractive guy within a five-mile radius. Not surprisingly, Dex seemed really into her, too. Sometimes Lili felt a little jealous of her laid-back friend's easy rapport with guys. It must come from hanging out with her brother's friends and Tri Fitzpatrick all the time, she mused. Speaking of whom, the poor guy had turned a sickening shade of green when he found out about A. A.'s Internet amigo the other day. She wondered if Tri knew that A. A. was finally going to get to meet the famous "laxjock" next week. Ashley joked that he was probably some fat, home-schooled loser, but somehow Lili didn't think so.

"C'mon, pick another card," Dex was urging, his bright blue eyes fixed on A. A., who fluttered her eyelashes at him in response.

A. A. put a slim hand on the deck and pulled out another one, just as they heard a loud cough right behind them. They turned around to see Lauren standing outside of their little circle. She was wearing a cool vintage-looking jumpsuit and a pair of ass-kicking knee-high boots that Lili immediately added to her own wish list. The Ashleys immediately crowded around her.

"Hi, pretty!" Ashley said, calling Lauren over. "Sit *here*. Scootch over, Li," she went on bossily, patting the barstool next to her. And even though Lili knew Ashley's friendship was as fake as her "Stella McCartney" jacket, she still felt a bit jealous of all the attention Ashley was heaping on Lauren. It was one thing to befriend the girl to get a guy. It was another thing to make her your new BFF completely.

"Thanks for sending the car," Lili said politely, as she took one single cashew nut from a wooden bowl on the counter and ate it. "Omigod. I'm so full," she announced.

"What time's wheels up?" Ashley asked with a yawn. She always had to make sure everyone knew she'd been on a private jet before and that this was just an ordinary event.

"Mom's just checking with the pilot now," said Lauren, just as Trudy Page entered the room.

"Welcome, girls!" Trudy gushed, planting effusive kisses on each Ashley's cheek. "So wonderful to have you all here!" she trilled, waving her hand so that they couldn't help but notice the massive rock on her finger and the row of diamond bracelets that glittered in the sunlight and threatened to blind them all.

Lili wrinkled her nose at the showy display of jewelry. Lauren's mom was a trip. She looked like a Christmas tree: overdecorated and way too shiny.

Ashley seemed to think similarly. "Is that real fur?" she asked, motioning to the pouffy white collar on Trudy's pink velvet coat. "It's gorgeous," she added, her voice dripping with insincerity.

"Why, yes it is," Trudy beamed, totally clueless.

"Figured," Ashley smirked, shooting Lili and A. A. a look.

"Can we go now?" Lauren asked her mother, sounding just a bit whiny. Lili wondered if she'd noticed the exchange among the Ashleys.

"Of course. I just spoke to Captain Jim and they're all

ready for us," Trudy said. "Hello, Dexter. Could you make sure we're all set here before we leave?" she asked grandly.

"Sure thing, Mrs. P.," Dex said easily, wiping the counter and filling the dishwasher.

They left the lounge, passing two businessmen waiting for their helicopters, and walked out to the small tarmac. The airfield was filled with small six- to nine-seater planes, as well as a few sleek G5's.

Lili automatically looked toward the smaller planes. Her dad had a little prop plane that he used to fly the family to Napa on weekends, and surely this wouldn't be too different from that. They were just flying to L.A., after all.

But to her surprise Lauren led them all the way back, to the largest plane on the lot, a behemoth 747 with the YourTV logo emblazoned on the wing. A rolling staircase led to the open entry door, where a uniformed flight attendant waved from the top of the plank. Lili could feel her mouth hanging open and closed it quickly. Were these people for real? It was like an episode of *Your Fantabulous Life*, that cable show where ordinary people lived like celebrities for one day, complete with narration by a guy with a fake British accent.

They followed Lauren up the stairs. Dex walked in front of them, and Lili elbowed A. A., who'd been staring at his butt for too long to be polite.

A gray-haired pilot emerged from the cockpit.

"Morning, ma'am." He nodded, tipping his hat to Trudy. "It's a beautiful day for a flight; we'll be in Los Angeles in no time. Hello, girls. Welcome aboard YourJet."

"*Our* jet?" asked Ashley, turning to the other girls and raising an eyebrow.

"It's a joke," Lauren explained. "Dad's company is YourTV, so he named the plane YourJet. He also calls our house YourHouse. Dad's a little corny."

"Oh. Can I have YourGucci, then?" A. A. asked with a smile, looking like she was thoroughly enjoying herself.

"You're funny," Lili deadpanned. "Get it? YourFunny?" The others looked blank. Lili shook her head. "Forget it."

They climbed aboard what looked like the most tricked-out airplane in existence. The main cabin was designed like a proper living room, with fluffy white couches that Lili could swear were made from the same beast that provided the fur for Trudy Page's coat, several glass coffee tables, a mammoth flat-screen television, and an entertainment console with DVD and satellite receivers.

"Wow," A. A. said simply.

Lili nodded, glad that she didn't have to say it.

"When we rode our plane to Tokyo, they had all the magazines and snacks we'd requested beforehand on board already." Ashley sniffed, still trying to look as if the jet was no big deal while she looked around for the remote control to the TV.

Funny how Ashley said "our plane," even though Lili knew from her parents that technically, the Spencers only had a membership in a private jet club and didn't own their own set of wings.

"What would you like?" Lauren asked graciously. "We've got everything on hand." She showed them the well-stocked pantry in the galley kitchen. It was like an upscale newsstand in there, complete with the latest issues of all the fashion and style bibles as well as the celebrity newsweeklies, including the international editions of *OK!*, *Hello!* and *Paris Match*.

Lili hesitated at first, noticing that Ashley had taken a seat on the couch and was looking around disdainfully with her arms crossed. But then she caught A. A.'s eye. The tall girl smiled gleefully and Lili grinned back, and soon the two of them began grabbing magazines, potato chips, candy, and sodas with abandon, losing all their cool in their rush to accumulate as much stuff as possible.

"I'm not hungry," Ashley said with a pout.

Lili shrugged and joined A.A on the couch with their bounty—every kind of candy imaginable, including gourmet chocolate bars from Switzerland and Belgium, a mouth-watering assortment of potato, tortilla, and soy chips in every flavor, and a dizzying variety of popcorn and puffed corn snacks. Lili thought she'd died and gone to snack heaven. As if that wasn't enough, Lauren asked the flight attendant to make them a round of strawberry smoothies.

"Omigod. Did we already take off?" asked Lili, looking out the window and noticing that they were already above the clouds. She hadn't felt a rumble or heard anything to mark their ascent.

"Five minutes ago," Lauren replied with a smile, opening a small, exquisite-looking brown cardboard box tied with an orange ribbon and showing them the row of creamy truffles inside. "They're Michel Richart. The best chocolates on the planet. My dad gets them flown in from France every week."

"Are you guys really going to eat all that?" Ashley asked accusingly, as A. A. tore open several different bags and canisters of chips and candy at once.

Lili would have answered, but she was too busy stuffing fistfuls of delicious imported cheesy puffs into her mouth and chasing them down with hazelnut truffles. So what if Ashley thought she was a pig?

This was way too much fun to pass up.

18

FLYING HIGH

LIKE ASHLEY, A. A. HAD BEEN ON A PRIVATE JET before. Her mother always seemed to be able to hitch rides with her richer friends on their planes when they went on vacation. But she'd never seen one as nice as this, and she wasn't afraid to say so. When Lauren had first invited them on the trip, she'd almost backed out because she was supposed to finally meet laxjock that weekend, but she was glad to have postponed it.

She planned to meet him next Friday instead. It was the same afternoon as the Miss Gamble's dance, but she didn't want to put him off any longer. She figured she could slip out once it got started, and on the off chance things didn't work out, she could always go back to the dance and . . . dance her heartache away, she supposed.

A. A. was curious about Lauren—she couldn't quite

figure the girl out. Why was she so keen on becoming their friend? Sure, everyone in class would kill to be one of them. But had Lauren truly forgotten how Ashley had treated her over the years? A. A. still remembered how in the third grade Ashley had made Lauren keep a "report card," where Ashley would give her "grades" and dole out punishments (lunch money embezzlement, hard pinches) if Lauren fell behind.

Of course, looking at the two of them now, sitting side by side, you'd think nothing like that had ever happened. They were leafing through a European fashion magazine together, while Lili ate cheesy poufs like there was no tomorrow. Sure, Ashley was pulling her usual seen-it-all-before act, but A. A. could tell she was pretty awed by the whole shebang. It was hard not to be.

"So glad to see you've made yourselves at home," Lauren's mom said, walking in wearing an Hermès towel around her shoulders. Her hair was wet and clipped back from her forehead. "Don't mind me, I'm just here for a glass of champagne. Can't keep Didier waiting!" she added gaily.

"Your mom travels with her own stylist?" Lili asked incredulously, taking a break from her no-trans-fats snackathon.

Lauren looked up from her magazine. "Sometimes."

A. A. watched her friends process this information, and she wondered when Ashley would casually mention that her mom never left San Francisco without her own entourage either.

"It's very convenient. When we went to Tokyo, we brought our chef with us," Ashley said.

"How big *is* this thing?" A. A. had to ask. "Don't tell me there's a salon and spa back there."

"I guess it is a pretty big plane," Lauren said almost apologetically. "No spa, but there is a Jacuzzi tub in one of the bathrooms. Dad has another smaller plane that he uses more. This one is the SUV."

"You guys have *two* jets?" exclaimed Lili.

"Three, actually," Trudy said merrily, as the flight attendant capped off her bubbling glass. "The G5 for cross-country, this one for European and Asia-Pacific flights, and a little one just for short trips. We were going to take the Citation, but it's being maintained."

There was nothing even Ashley could say to top that, and the room was silent until A. A. got up. "Where's the bathroom?" she asked, crumpling an empty bag of the tastiest Japanese rice crackers she'd ever eaten. She'd have to ask Lauren where to get more of them.

"There's one up front and two aft," Lauren answered.

"Thanks," she said, walking to the back of the plane. There were a bunch of closed doors in the back and she pushed one open, hoping it was the lavatory. Instead she'd stumbled into some sort of command-control room, with a bank of television screens, several computers, and an old-fashioned jukebox in the corner.

"Can I help you?" a voice asked, and Dex rolled into view, seated in one of those fancy ergonomic office chairs and wearing huge Bose headphones. He took off the headphones, and his face broke into one of those piercing smiles that belonged in a poster on the wall of every girl's bedroom.

A. A. had wondered where he'd disappeared to once they were in the air. "Oh, sorry. I didn't mean to bother you. I was just looking for the bathroom. I guess this isn't it," she said with a smile.

"It's the second door on the left," he told her.

"Thanks." A. A. nodded. She lingered by the doorway, wanting to hang out just a little more. "What is all this?" she asked, looking at what appeared to be dozens of television screens.

"The most popular videos on our site," he explained, pointing to the nearest screen. "We get thousands a day, and most of it is just junk. I'm trying to come up with a better way to filter it. There's a continuous stream of uploads. If something catches my eye, I move it to the recommended list."

"You can keep track of all this?" A. A. asked.

"Nah, I'm just doing a little bit of development for

Lauren's dad," said Dex, looking modest. "Hey, wanna see something cool?"

"Sure." A. A. nodded, walking closer. "Another card trick?" she teased.

"Better," Dex promised. He opened a drawer and removed a pair of dark sunglasses. "Put these on," he urged, handing them over carefully. Their fingers brushed as A. A. accepted them, and an electric current zipped up her spine. He was so cute, looking at her so intently as she tried them on.

"Okay. So now what?" she asked. They seemed like a pair of ordinary sunglasses to her. Did they give her Superman's X-ray vision? Not as far as she could tell.

"Look around. Look at me," Dex directed. "That should be enough." He removed them from her face gently. Then he took a wire that led from the computer and slid the jack into a hidden slot on the hinge of the frame.

"It's a camera," he explained. "A video camera. We're hoping to do this thing on YourTV where people can video-tape their whole lives. Every person you've ever met. Everywhere you've ever been. It's called lifelogging." He typed in some keystrokes and called up a video on the screen in front of him. It showed the room as A. A. had seen it, and Dex's smiling face, as well as a date in the corner. "They're not available to the public yet. Some kind of issue with the battery. But one day . . ."

"That is so ace," A. A. said.

"Thanks. I built it," said Dex modestly. He pushed up his sleeve, and A. A. noticed a *Speed Racer* tattoo on his forearm.

A. A. hitched herself up on the desk, crossing her long legs and feeling more and more comfortable in his presence. "Lauren said she's known you since she was little."

"That's 'cause I've been working with her dad since I was eleven," Dex told her, swiveling back to the row of screens. "Back when he was still just getting his PhD."

"So you're a computer geek," teased A. A.

"Hey—I coach the Gregory Hall lacrosse team! I wasn't too bad myself when I was there," Dex protested. "Not bad for an old guy."

"You're not old. You can't be more than what—twenty?" A. A. guessed.

"I was kidding. I'm actually only seventeen," said Dex. "I just graduated in the spring."

He didn't seem to mind her hanging out, but A. A. didn't want to impose any longer. Besides, she really did need to pee.

When she returned to the main cabin, the lights were dark and the girls were watching a new movie that hadn't even been released yet. Another YourTV perk, she guessed correctly.

"Where did you disappear to?" Ashley whispered.

A. A. shrugged. She was still thinking about what Dex had told her. He was seventeen years old, not twenty as she'd thought. He coached the lacrosse team. He had a *Speed Racer* tattoo on his forearm. He was super computer-savvy. Okay, so maybe fixing a virus on her home page wasn't the same thing as inventing the world's coolest video camera. And tons of guys liked *Speed Racer*. And played lacrosse.

But when she'd told laxjock she had to postpone because she was going out of town, he'd admitted he was relieved because he would be away that weekend too. But if he was laxjock, how come he didn't recognize her from her online photo? Maybe because it was in black-and-white and she wasn't wearing a ton of makeup right now? Or maybe he didn't expect to meet "hollabackgirl" among a group of preteens.

A. A. thought of how hot Dex looked with his sharp white button-down shirt tucked into his straight-leg jeans. He was exactly what she pictured laxjock would look like. But it was ridiculous. Dex couldn't be laxjock, could he?

Could he?

19

ONE OF THESE THINGS IS NOT LIKE THE OTHERS

S O THIS WAS WHAT HAVING FRIENDS WAS like. Lauren felt warm and cozy as she sat wedged in between Lili and Ashley, not quite believing she was finally in their company at last. They were sharing a tub of buttery, salty-sweet kettle corn, eyes glued to the screen where the dazzling hero of next summer's huge blockbuster was saving a screaming girl from several monstrous beasts. A. A. finally returned from the bathroom. Lauren was glad. A. A. had been gone for so long she was worried that she'd fallen out of the plane or something.

"Doesn't he look just like Billy Reddy?" Ashley asked, during a lull in the movie.

"Totally," agreed Lili, her cheeks full of popcorn. That

girl was small but she could eat, Lauren thought.

"A bit," A. A. said, a faraway look in her eye. "Or maybe Dex. Don't you think he kind of looks like Dex?" Which was an odd thing to say, since the star onscreen was dark-haired and dark-eyed and looked nothing at all like Dex. But Lauren could spot a Dexaholic a mile away. The girl was definitely smitten. Too bad Dex already had a girlfriend and didn't mess around with jailbait.

"A. A., you're delusional as usual," Ashley snapped. "We should call Billy," she suggested. "Tell him what he's missing. You guys are such good friends, right, Lauren? You should have invited him to join us today."

Lauren froze. "We can't use our cell phones up here," she said quickly. "And Daddy doesn't like us to use the air phone. I could get in trouble. Besides, Billy doesn't like to shop." Lauren had no idea if that was true, but she figured most boys hated shopping, so it was a safe assumption.

Ashley pouted but didn't push it, and Lauren felt relieved. For a while there, when she and A. A. had bonded over their love for dark chocolate and Lili had complimented her on her shoes, and even Ashley had made a point of sitting next to her, Lauren had felt that maybe they really liked her. But Ashley's question brought that fantasy crashing down to earth. They were hanging out with her only because Ashley thought she would introduce them to Billy Reddy—a prize

Lauren intended to keep dangling just out of reach.

Once Ashley met Billy, Lauren had the distinct impression that Ashley would have no more use for her and would kick her off the top of the social ladder. Besides, what if she took them to his lacrosse game and Billy had no idea who she was? Sure, he'd invited her to come see him play. But maybe he invited anyone he met. He was probably just being nice. She would have to stall their meeting for as long as she could.

"What's Billy's favorite movie?" Lili wanted to know. They had lost interest in the onscreen adventure once their favorite topic of discussion came up.

"Uh . . . *Nightmare Before Christmas*," Lauren said, because it was Dex's favorite movie.

"Aw. That's so sweet." Ashley sighed. "Quick Q. Do you think he'd prefer strawberry or mango?"

Lauren shrugged and thought it was safe to say she had no idea. "You guys, you're missing the best part," she said, motioning to the movie. The girls turned to the screen for one second, registered that the handsome hero was professing his undying love to the hapless heroine, and quickly turned back to one another.

"Why do you want to know?" asked A. A. "Are you sending Billy a fruit basket?"

"So I know what lip gloss to wear when he kisses me, duh!" Ashley cackled. A. A. laughed, but Lili made a face that showed she thought that was totally gross. Lauren was glad to see that someone else felt just as conflicted about kissing boys as she did. Ashley had said she couldn't imagine being thirteen and never-been-kissed, but Lauren thought she could probably wait at least that long.

"He doesn't have a girlfriend, right, Lauren? You told us he didn't," Lili said in an almost accusatory tone.

She had told them that, not knowing whether it was true or not, and apparently it was the wrong answer—the grapevine had it that Billy was dating some Reed Prep freshman—but Lauren had thought it was better to say Billy was unattached, so the Ashleys would think they had a chance with him and keep Lauren around for longer.

"No, no girlfriend. I told you he broke up with her," Lauren said, keeping her fingers crossed behind her back.

"Everything okay in here? Everyone having fun?" asked her mother, popping in again for the hundredth time, her hair now perfectly coiffed. Lauren wished her mom wouldn't act so eager to please.

Like that bit about calling Dex by his full name earlier, something Trudy never did. Her mother was just as nervous about hosting the Ashleys as she was, and Lauren wished she would relax. That was the impossible thing about the Ashleys. Even if you secretly hated them, you still wanted them to like you.

So far, everything seemed to be going well enough. They did seem like they were having fun, and they were impressed by everything so far. At least A. A. and Lili were. It was hard to tell how Ashley felt. Lauren had felt a little left out earlier, when the Ashleys showed up for the day all wearing the same thing. They were like the world's corniest girl band. Why did they all have to match all the time? Lauren was relieved when they took off the coats and sunglasses and she saw they were all wearing different things underneath—Ashley in a pale cashmere sweater and wool shorts, Lili in a tunic blouse and roomy oversize cardigan over leggings, and A. A. in a simple black turtleneck and black pants.

"We're going to be landing soon," she told them, zapping off the television screen and making an effort to tidy up the discarded candy wrappers, empty chocolate boxes, and half-eaten bags of chips that littered the floor. She noticed that none of the Ashleys offered to lift a finger. Ashley had even put her riding boots on top of Lauren's dad's cherished cherrywood coffee table. Lauren wished she could tell Ashley that no one put their feet up on the table, but she didn't have the courage.

"We're here?" asked Ashley. Lauren noticed her nodding meaningfully to the other two.

"Could you excuse us for a sec?" Lili asked. Lauren watched as the three of them grabbed their Fendi bags and matching F-logo carryalls and disappeared to the back of the plane. Should she join them? But she wasn't invited. But wasn't it her plane? Lauren felt stymied once again. Every time she thought she had finally cracked the Ashleys' code—looking perfect, check, having cool stuff to show off, check, acting like the whole world revolved around you, check—they added another clause to the rulebook.

A few minutes later the Ashleys emerged. Gone were the thick sweaters and warm boots. Ashley was in a tank top with an A-line miniskirt and Prada flip-flops, Lili was wearing an airy spaghetti-strap sundress over a tissue-thin T-shirt and cork mules, and A. A. wore a Lilly Pulitzer polo with Bermuda shorts and Chloé flats. Even their complexions looked different—they looked *tan*.

"Did you guys find a tanning booth back there?" Lauren joked, trying not to feel too excluded. She wished she'd remembered to keep her Mystic appointment last week. Maintenance on her new look was a lot of work, and she had a hard time keeping up. Already her roots were growing in curly—the horror!

"Tan in a can," explained A. A., showing Lauren the aerosol sunless tanner. "Here, you want some?" she asked, spritzing a thick mist on Lauren's face before she could reply.

Lauren coughed and waved A. A. off, but it was too late. She felt her face turning orange.

"You just can't wear San Francisco clothes in L.A.,"
Lili declared as she folded up her bulky clothes. "It's not
just a different climate, it's a different style sensibility."
She expertly powdered her cheeks with bronzer to cover up
any streaks.

"Totally," A. A. agreed, stuffing the self-tanner back into
her purse. "It's, like, year-round summer. But you can wear
your San Francisco clothes in New York."

"Duh," said Lili.

"Do you mind if we just leave our things here?" Ashley
asked. She gave Lauren the old up-and-down, taking in the
belted jumpsuit and the thick-soled boots. "Aren't you going
to be hot in that?" she smirked.

Lauren hoped it wasn't going to be one of those eighty-
eight-degree SoCal days. She kicked herself for not thinking
to bring a change of clothes like they had. Then again, they
could have been nice enough to tell her what the plan was.

But that was the thing. The Ashleys weren't nice. They
weren't her friends. She'd gotten past the velvet rope at the
front of the club, but she had yet to make it inside the VIP
room. She wasn't one of them. At least, not yet.

20

GIRLS JUST WANNA HAVE FUN

T WAS ONLY AN HOUR TO LOS ANGELES ON A private plane, but for Ashley, it couldn't end fast enough. She'd had to take a backseat while onboard, since she was a guest on Lauren's plane. It wasn't like she could stop A. A. and Lili from making total fools of themselves, stuffing their faces full of chocolate and chips and oohing and ahhing over everything inside that tacky flying McMansion. Now that they were back on the ground, Ashley felt more like herself again. In command.

"Where are we?" A. A. asked, shielding her eyes from the glare on the tarmac. It was a beautiful, cloudless, blue-sky day. A soft wind whispered through the gently swaying palm trees.

"Santa Monica," said Lauren, a thin sheen of perspiration on her face already, Ashley was glad to see. "It's the nearest private airport to Beverly Hills."

"Ladies," Dex announced, opening the door of an immaculately preserved cherry-red vintage Cadillac convertible that was parked by the airplane.

"Great car," Lili gushed.

"Thanks," Lauren said. "My dad's a bit of a car freak. He bought it from some famous actor. He wanted to send a limo for us, but I thought you guys would like this better. It's really hard to find a vintage Caddy in great condition."

Ashley was still determined not to be impressed by anything Lauren showed her, but now her resolve was weakening, especially at the sight of the beautiful red car. So what. It was only a car. "Isn't vintage just another word for 'used'?" Ashley asked.

Lauren looked relieved when A. A. immediately began asking about the doodads on the dashboard, and she showed them how the old-fashioned radio worked.

Ashley climbed into the backseat next to Lili and Trudy while Lauren and A. A. sat up front. She noticed A. A. was paying Dex a lot of attention. He was definitely a cutie, but, hello, a little old for them, she thought. But then, A. A. was *supposed* to be experienced, so maybe she could handle it.

Dex drove smoothly through the streets of Santa Monica, past the boardwalk, where Ashley could see the waves cresting and armies of people gathered on the beach. There were families having picnics, couples riding bikes, groups of friends tossing Frisbees. A giant Ferris wheel towered over the whole scene, and the air smelled like hot dogs. Lauren was still blabbing on and on about how the actor had given her family a tour of the set of his latest movie, and A. A. and Lili were totally eating it all up. How long did she have to listen to this girl yak?

Not very long, she decided, spotting a shaggy-haired guy in a loose-fitting top walking on the sidewalk and gasped. "Look! It's that guy from *So You Think You Can Dance!*" she shrieked, bringing Lauren's monologue to a halt. "The cute one!"

"Omigod. Is it?" Lili asked, standing up from her seat as well.

"Not a chance. Fooled you." Ashley laughed, glad to have caught their attention. In retaliation Lili pelted her with yogurt raisins she'd taken from the plane.

"Are we going to see any celebrities?" A. A. asked eagerly, craning her neck around madly.

"A. A., you see celebs all the time," growled Ashley. Did she have to remind A. A. that her mother was practically a celebrity herself?

"Those are just San Francisco celebrities," A. A. replied, with an eye roll of her own. "Some romance writer and some geezer actor. I want to see Daphne Shepard and Venice Westin."

By then all three Ashleys were standing in the open-top

car, and they began to attract a lot of attention in the slow-moving traffic. Ashley started waving and blowing kisses to anyone who beeped at them, and Lili and A. A. soon followed suit. Lauren, Ashley was glad to note, was sitting rigidly and looking like she was not quite sure what to do.

"Hey, it's the StripHall Queens—turn it up!" Ashley ordered as the radio began blasting the popular song with the heavy bass line. The three girls immediately began their synchronized dancing, the result of years of dance-team dominance. The Ashleys had made nationals last year.

"Who's sexiest girl in the whole . . . ," they yelled, each pointing to herself during the chorus. "Who's the sexiest girl in the whole . . . world?"

"C'mon, Lauren, dance," A. A. said, pulling her up to stand. Lauren danced, but she didn't know any of the moves and settled for bobbing her head while the Ashleys mimed taking their clothes off. There was a frenzy of beeping and whooping when A. A. accidentally showed a little more skin than she intended to the crowd on the sidewalk during a vigorous over-the-head sequence.

"Girls, sit down," Dex ordered, as the girls fell backward when the car lurched forward at the green light. "I'm going to get a ticket."

"Aw, let them have their fun," called Trudy from the backseat. "You're only young once."

True enough, Mrs. P., Ashley thought. *Although you'd never think it from the way you dress.*

Ashley sat back down, fanning her face with her hands, energized by the impromptu showcase. The song had ended and traffic began to move again. She noticed that they had left the streets of Santa Monica and had entered Beverly Hills proper.

"We're on Rodeo," she said, elbowing Lili. The glittering avenue was famed for its high-end retail emporiums and was one of Ashley's favorite places in the world. The storefronts were as polished and sleek as the shoppers walking on the sidewalks.

Dex drove up to a building with jaunty red canopies over the windows. "Barneys. Your stop, ma'am," he said to Trudy, who climbed out of the car.

Ashley prepared to follow her out, but Trudy had already slammed the door. "You girls have fun now. Dex is going to keep an eye on you. Lauren, honey, don't spend it all in one place, okay?" Trudy instructed, handing her daughter a platinum credit card.

Then Dex revved up the engine and they were on their way again. Ashley looked back longingly at the store, wondering why they weren't going there. They drove past a host of elegant boutiques. Bulgari. Louis Vuitton. Tiffany. Gucci. Versace. Valentino. Then they were out of Rodeo Drive entirely.

Finally she couldn't stand it anymore. "Aren't we stopping here?" she asked plaintively when they passed Saks Fifth Avenue.

"We're not going to Rodeo Drive," replied Lauren.

"Oh? Why not? I thought we were shopping in Beverly Hills," Ashley said with a toss of her head.

"Sure, any tourist could shop on Rodeo," said Lauren in the condescending tone that Ashley recognized as her own. "But we're going somewhere better."

"What's better than Beverly Hills?" A. A. wanted to know.

Lili shrugged.

Did Lauren know something they didn't? Were they really going to get schooled in shopping from a girl who'd spent her whole life to this point in hand-me-down sweaters?

Ashley squirmed in her seat. Lauren was probably going to take them somewhere really obvious, like the Beverly Center or something. But there was nothing she could do about it. Outside, the scenery began to change from the glitzy streets of Beverly Hills to the more gritty environs of Los Angeles proper. Ashley couldn't understand why they had to leave Rodeo Drive without stopping at even *one* store.

She reached over and pinched Lili out of boredom.

"Ow!" Lili yelped, slapping her hand away. "What was that for?"

"Nothing." Ashley sighed. Even watching Lili jump out of her seat wasn't as fun as she thought it would be.

"Um, hello," she said to Lauren.

"Yes?" Lauren asked.

Ashley spoke slowly, enunciating each syllable, the better to get her point across. "Where exactly are we going? This is not what we signed up for. Ow!" she squealed, feeling a shooting pain on her arm as Lili pinched her back. "No fair. You have a death grip."

Ashley pinched Lili back and Lili did the same until both girls were covered in red welts on their arms and legs.

"I promise you'll like it," Lauren said desperately.

"Promises are made to be broken," snapped Ashley. "Dude, turn this car around and let's go back to Saks."

"Sorry, miss. Got to go where Lauren tells me," Dex said evenly.

"You guys!" A. A. suddenly cut in. "It's DAPHNE SHEPARD!" she screamed, waving madly toward a wisp of a girl with a blond bob who was making her way quickly down the street, holding a gigantic Balenciaga bag that was almost as big as her torso.

Ashley immediately pushed Lili away, and the two of them practically climbed all over each other to get a look.

"Oh. My. God. It *is* Daphne," said Lili, gnawing on her bead necklace in excitement.

"Stop the car!" Ashley ordered. "Now!"

Dex stopped the car.

Whether it was Ashley's sharp, no-nonsense tone, or whether they had finally arrived where Lauren was taking them, Ashley didn't know. But she didn't dwell on it too much, since she had to see where Daphne was headed, and more important, what she was going to buy.

21

SHOPPING IS A COMPETITIVE SPORT, AND LILI ALWAYS GOES FOR GOLD

L ILI ALMOST TRIPPED ON HER CORK WEDGES getting out of the convertible in her haste to follow Daphne Shepard. The star had been walking on a charming, tree-lined street filled with small, vibrant, one-of-a-kind boutiques, and it was hard to keep an eye on her, since it looked to Lili as if every girl on the street was a Daphne clone. They were all wearing fluttery camisoles and denim shorts as tiny as their sunglasses and handbags were enormous.

"This is Robertson Boulevard," Lauren was saying. "My sister goes to UCLA, and she told me this is where everyone in L.A. really shops."

Lili nodded approvingly. There was a mellow, laid-back

vibe to the place, with nary a Nikon-wielding tourist anywhere. "Where'd she go?" she asked, not seeing Daphne
anywhere.

"I think she went over there," A. A. said, leading the way
to a candy-colored boutique across the street. They tried to
get inside but were stymied by a mob of shoppers waiting
behind a velvet rope in front of the store. The line was so
long it snaked all the way down the block and around the next
corner.

Lili recognized the store as one of those celebrity emporiums, having read all about it in her favorite tabloids. The
trendy boutique and its wares—T-shirts proclaiming alle-
giances in the current celebrity feud, the jeans of the
moment (which right now were neon-colored skinny), and
Gwen Stefani's Harajuku Lovers line of plastic tote bags—
were as famous as the celebrities who shopped there.

"WTF?" asked Ashley, determined to push her way through.

Lili had to agree. She'd never heard of a line to get inside
a store. Maybe this was why they called L.A. la-la land.
Everything in the city seemed larger than life. The sky was
bluer. The cars were bigger. Everyone on the street looked
like a movie star. Even the stores were run like *nightclubs*, Lili
thought, which reminded her of the mixer and all the items
she had yet to tick off her to-do list. It was a week away. Not
a problem. She took out her cell and dialed a well-known

caterer her mother always worked with. She could at least be productive if they were forced to stand in line.

"I need hot and cold hors d'oeuvres, a sushi bar, and a buffet station for about a hundred people," she said. "Fax the menu to my cell phone for my approval. Thanks."

Food? Check.

"This is *ridonculous!*" Ashley announced, jostling for the best spot like she always did. Lili secretly enjoyed seeing the pained look on Ashley's face. It was so rare for her to experience any adversity. No one ever said no to Ashley. She didn't know what "no" meant; to Ashley "no" only meant "not now" or "maybe later."

"Excuse you!" screeched an annoyed shopper who was wearing all the season's trends—patent platform wedges, metallic bag, and argyle vest—in one outfit.

"Get to the back of the line!" another complained, angrily pushing up the sleeves on her balloon tunic blouse.

"Watch it," threatened A. A., standing up straight and staring down a fashion victim who'd poked an elbow in her direction. It was good to have A. A. around at a time like this. She didn't take any crap from anyone.

It looked like they would never get inside until Lauren caught up to them. Their new friend had lagged behind to talk to Dex, and of course, none of the Ashleys had bothered to wait for her. Lili couldn't help but think she looked a tad amused as she approached. "What are you guys doing back here?" Lauren asked.

"Um, because there's a line?" Ashley snapped.

Lauren sighed. "C'mon, follow me. They know me here," she told them, walking all the way to the front as if she did it all the time.

Lili exchanged we've-got-to-see-this looks with the other Ashleys, but they trotted dutifully after Lauren, not wanting to get left behind just in case she was telling the truth.

"Hi, Cherry," Lauren called, trading air kisses with the skinny girl in a faux-vintage Led Zeppelin T-shirt and cropped red jeans manning the door. "These are my friends. Can we go in?"

"Of course. Hi, girls!" The salesgirl smiled. "Omigod, it's like madness today. I think there was a feature on E! this weekend or something," she said, unlocking the velvet rope and waving them inside.

Lili reached out and grabbed Ashley's hand and saw A. A. do the same to Ashley's other hand, and the three of them ran inside the store without bothering to thank Lauren.

"Where is she?" Lili despaired, not finding Daphne's sleek blond head anywhere in the store. But she lost interest in star-spotting once she laid eyes on a rack of multicolored dresses. She saw Ashley eyeing the impressive shoe selection and A. A. piling on the jeans.

For a solid twenty minutes, Lili concentrated on finding the perfect dress for the dance. She knew exactly what she wanted: something on-trend but not trendy, something girly but not cutesy, something chic but also easy to wear that would allow her to move. She didn't want to spend the entire evening tugging on a too-short hemline or pushing up straps that kept falling. She chose several promising-looking options and disappeared into one of the dressing rooms in the back of the store.

A few minutes later she pried open the curtain so she could check herself out in the large mirror hanging in front of all the dressing rooms. The store seemed to encourage shoppers to model the items they'd selected, and she had to fight a bunch of gorgeous girls trying on an array of sexy backless tops to catch her reflection. She assessed herself in a lacy white eyelet number with a handkerchief hem.

Too Bo-Peep, Lili thought, shaking her head.

The next one was a black mod shift with a row of oversize buttons on the side.

Too costumey.

She put on the last one, a simple black jersey dress with spaghetti straps. It looked like nothing on the hanger, but Lili had a feeling it was one of those dresses that were deceptively simple but effortlessly chic. Once she saw herself in the mirror she knew.

This was the one.

The dress skimmed her slim hips, and the soft cowl neckline showed off her delicate collarbone. It was perfect. It was hers. She did a little jiggle of happiness from a shopping high.

Then she heard the sound of curtains being pushed aside with a flourish and watched with a sickening sense of foreboding as Ashley pranced out of her dressing room. Her shopping high disappeared and she crashed back down to earth. Ashley was wearing the exact same dress.

"Omigod!" they chorused. Lili felt better when both of them began to laugh after they realized what they'd done. But she stopped laughing when she heard what Ashley said next.

"You are such a biter," Ashley teased.

"Me? You're the one who always bites off me," Lili replied, trying to keep her voice light. She was the one who'd suggested they all get Fendi Spy bags for back-to-school, and look what happened.

Lili noticed A. A. walking over to referee, like she always did. "You look great in that, Lil," A. A. said. "You too, Ash," she added, almost as an afterthought.

Lili had no idea why Ashley would want the dress, since the stark black color made her look totally washed out. Not that she would ever tell Ashley that.

"Yeah, you guys both look awesome," Lauren agreed,

coming over and adding her two cents, although no one paid attention.

"I was thinking of wearing it to the dance," Ashley declared, her hands on her hips.

"Me too," countered Lili, her voice tight. "I found it first." She felt the tension in the room rise as they surreptitiously checked each other out in the mirror. No one said anything for a long time, until Ashley's cool voice broke the silence.

"You know, Lil, I think it looks great on you, as long as you're comfortable showing so much skin," Ashley cooed. "It's a little hoochie."

"Are you serious?" asked Lili. She grimaced. Was Ashley right? Was it skank city? Now that she thought about it, it was a little daring. Or was Ashley just playing her?

"I think she looks great in it," Lauren burst in. "You really do, Lil." Not that Lili cared what Lauren thought at all. This was between her and Ashley.

"Oh, definitely," Ashley agreed, as if Lauren was being completely reasonable. "I don't think she looks like a baby prostitute at all."

"You did not just call Lili a baby ho." A. A. laughed. A. A. wasn't going to be any help, Lili despaired. She was Switzerland whenever it came to style skirmishes and never got involved in her friends' jousting for top position.

"I don't know," Lili said, as she returned to the sanctuary of her own dressing room, a troubled look on her face. She suddenly wished she had gone shopping alone.

"Yeah, I'm not getting it either," said Ashley triumphantly, in a voice that implied *case closed*.

We'll see about that, Lili thought.

22

DON'T JUDGE A GIRL UNTIL
YOU'VE WALKED A MILE
IN HER CHOOS

WHILE LILI HAD BEEN BUSY ADMIR-
ing herself in the mirror, Ashley
turned over the price tag. Six hundred
dollars. She was shocked. Not because of the price, which was
expensive, sure, but in keeping with the many designer
clothes in her closet. She was shocked because it was only
then that she realized that there was no way she could afford
to buy it. Her mother had taken away her credit cards. The
only card she had in her Fendi wallet was a debit card linked
to her allowance account. Which only had two hundred and
fifty dollars in it. Enough to cover lunch, maybe a pair of
jeans if she foud some Superfine ones on sale. But that was
about it.

If she couldn't have the dress, she couldn't very well let Lili walk out with it either. Thank the L that Lili was so easy to manipulate. She certainly wasn't going to spend six large after Ashley had called it the h-word. Ashley walked back into her dressing room feeling much better.

She left all the silly, overpriced clothes in a messy pile on the floor of the dressing room and walked around the store again. This place was such a rip. Now that she remembered she was effectively poor for the day, she had lost all interest in shopping. Well, maybe she could find something in the cheapo tables up front. Usually Ashley avoided the trinkets-and-candles section of the pricey designer boutiques. She knew they were there only so that those on smaller budgets could feel better about themselves. As if a ten-dollar key ring counted.

Then she found something. A gold plastic goblet decorated with fake jewel stones and emblazoned with the word PIMP in multicolored letters. A Pimp Cup. Hilarious. And it was only eighteen dollars. Score! She grinned, without realizing that this was exactly the kind of consolation purchase the tables were supposed to encourage. She brought it to the register, where A. A. was paying for a stack of Serfontaine jeans and a bunch of T-shirts.

"Do you think it's cute?" A. A. asked, holding up a "Little Miss Bossy" T-shirt.

"So cute." Ashley nodded.

"That's all you're getting?" A. A. looked curiously at the Pimp Cup.

"I didn't like anything else," Ashley lied. She would really have to let her mom have it when they got home. Her whole day was *ruined*.

Lili came up empty-handed as well, although Lauren appeared with a bunch of shopping bags.

"Cool!" said Lauren, pointing at Ashley's Pimp Cup. "I want one!"

Of course you do, Ashley thought, as Lauren ran back to the bargain bins near the storefront window to grab her own.

The four of them exited the store, lingering on the sidewalk, where the line to get inside had grown exponentially since they'd arrived. The midday sun was beating down mercilessly, and Ashley was really starting to feel the heat, which prickled on her fair skin.

"Gross, I think I'm sweating," she said, misting her face with an aerosol Evian can. She'd picked up the habit from when her family was in the Riviera over spring break last year. "Anyone else want a spritz?"

"Pass it over." A. A. nodded, taking the can and giving herself a healthy dose.

"Girls don't sweat, they glow," Lili said, quoting from

their gym teacher as she sprayed herself with mist. Physical education at Miss Gamble's was a bit of a joke. The other day they had learned how to play croquet and other "lawn sports."

Lauren accepted the Evian mineral spray from Lili and pressed the button, releasing a sharp burst of water. She coughed and blinked, to the other girls' amusement. Ashley smirked. You can take the geek out of the comic book convention, but you can't take the comic book convention out of the geek.

"Where to next, Lauren?" asked A. A.

"Yeah, where are we going now?" Lili echoed.

But before Lauren could answer, Ashley decided that it was time to end Lauren's tour of Los Angeles. "I think I saw Daphne go that way," she said, motioning to the store across the street. "I'm going over there," she added, fully expecting everyone to follow.

"That store does have the best shoe selection," Lauren agreed, taking off her sunglasses and squinting in the direction Ashley was pointing. "But I thought we should check out this sale down the street. They have good stuff if you're still looking for a dress to wear to the dance."

"I vote for shoes," A. A. decided.

"Well, I am still looking for a dress for the dance," Lili admitted, looking warily at Ashley and A. A. before sidling up to Lauren.

Ashley's eyes bugged out of her skull. Was Lili seriously going to ditch them to hang with Lauren? "Fine," she said, as if she wasn't bothered in the least. "It's not like you need my permission," she sniffed, rubbing it in because Lili looked like her permission was the very thing she wanted.

Lili colored. "We'll meet you for lunch in half an hour?"

Ashley shrugged and said something noncommittal as she began walking away, A. A. following right behind her.

"What's the deal with Lili lately?" Ashley asked as she pushed the glass door open so it tinkled as they entered the all-white boutique. "She's acting like she's not even our friend anymore. She's, like, *obsessed* with Lauren."

A. A. grunted but didn't respond. That was the problem with A. A.—you could never get her to trash-talk about their other best friend. Much.

They looked at the shelves of shoes. Lauren was right, the store had a dazzling array of the latest designer footwear. Ashley surveyed the goods: exquisite jeweled sandals by Giuseppe Zanotti, gorgeous peep-toe Carmen Ho pumps, yummy Tory Burch Reva flats with the gold disk on the toe.

"Love these," said A. A., snatching up a red patent-leather Jimmy Choo short boot from a nearby shelf and turning it over to check the price tag.

"Me too!" Ashley enthused, grabbing the other shoe.

"I know, aren't they great?" a sultry voice asked from behind.

Ashley turned around to see Daphne Shepard parading in the very same shoes. She looked even skinnier and prettier up close, with brilliant hazel eyes and a dazzling smile. Her tan was a delicious shade of buttery caramel, and her knees were as tiny as her elbows. She moved like a bird—all flutter and light. She smiled at the girls and turned to the clerk. "I'll take them."

Ashley pinched A. A. hard on the underside of her arm, and A. A. did the same to the underside of Ashley's arm, but neither of them said anything until Daphne left the store.

"That was so cool!" A. A. exhaled, releasing her grip. "Let's call Lili and tell her what she missed." She whipped out her cell.

"Let's not and say we did," said Ashley, grinning. Served her right for running off with Lauren.

"Don't be mean," A. A. admonished, dialing. "Huh. She's not picking up."

"Maybe she and Lauren ran off together."

A. A. put her phone away and waved at the salesgirl. "Can we get two of these?" she asked. "Sizes five and five and a half?"

The salesgirl returned with two lavender boxes, and Ashley kicked off her flats to try them on. Next to her, A. A. was doing the same. Ashley stood up and admired how the high heel elongated her calf. She would have to hide them from her mother, though—she was only allowed to wear two-and-a-half-inch heels until her thirteenth birthday.

"These shoes rock," she declared.

"We're totally getting them," A. A. agreed.

"Yes we are." Ashley nodded. Matching shoes was a trademark of the Ashleys. Then her face froze. She couldn't afford the shoes any more than she could afford that black dress from earlier, but if she just put it on hold, A. A. would ask why she had to do that, and she didn't want A. A. to know her allowance was restricted. If there was one thing Ashley couldn't stand, it was pity.

"How are we doing over here?" the salesgirl asked, coming over with an obsequious smile.

Ashley was about to offer an excuse, but before she could, A. A. handed her credit card to the clerk. "We'll take them. They're my treat."

"Are you sure?" Ashley asked, suddenly wishing she hadn't been so mean about laxjock. Even if he totally was a fat, homeschooled loser. Didn't A. A. ever watch any *Dateline*? Hello.

"C'mon, it's a birthday present," said A. A.

"My birthday's not for a couple of months," Ashley pointed out.

"And I should probably get Lili a pair too," A. A. added thoughtfully. "Her birthday was last week."

"Thanks, A." Ashley sighed. She sat back down on the couch, ruminating on her friend's unexpected generosity. Maybe if she told her mom they were a gift, she would be allowed to wear them.

Everyone always thought Ashley Spencer's life was beyond perfect, but sometimes even someone as perfect as Ashley Spencer couldn't get by without a little help from her friends.

23

WHAT A GIRL WANTS

AUREN WATCHED LILI WATCH HER FRIENDS walk away. Lili had chosen to hang out with her rather than the other two Ashleys! This was a good thing, right? Lili was also the one who had given her that unsolicited advice on how to get "in" with Ashley Spencer. Lili was the key. She was the weak link in the clique. If she could somehow get Lili to stop being Ashley's friend, that would create a tear in the very fabric of the Ashleys' existence. And the Ashleys didn't do tears.

But Lili looked like she was dearly regretting her decision to strike out on her own. She looked like she had just lost her best friend—which she had, sorta. Lauren had to act fast. "I think they have your dress at the store we're going to."

"What dress?" Lili asked. "I don't know what you're talking about."

Fine, be that way. This would take a little finessing. They

walked inside the store, which had several wooden tables piled high with every kind of designer T-shirt imaginable, at prices that would have bought dozens of Hanes three-packs.

"Ashley, what do you think of this?" Lauren asked, lifting up a rib-knit Henley.

"Why do you keep calling me Ashley?" Lili was looking at Lauren as if Lauren were a bug underneath a microscope.

"Uh, because it's your name?"

"I don't know if you've noticed, but I go by Lili now. You can call me Lili, you know. Everyone does," Lili huffed.

Lauren blushed. She had been too scared to call Ashley Li and Ashley Alioto by their cute nicknames. Only the cool girls in class—the SOAs—did so. She told Lili this.

"I never noticed," said Lili, shrugging. Lauren watched as she picked up a T-shirt that cost the same as Lauren's old digital camera. Her parents had saved for months to be able to afford it in the year before YourTV launched. It still amazed Lauren how casually some girls could spend a fortune on the most innocuous items. Who knew the right T-shirt cost so much? Even if her dad could afford to buy the whole store, Lauren was still nervous about spending money like water.

They shopped in silence, riffling through the stack of super-soft T-shirts, until Ashley Li—*Lili*—let out an exasperated sigh.

"Like, it's always about *her*, you know? What about me?" she said angrily. "I mean, I did find the dress first."

Lauren intuited that it was best not to respond. This was a great example of a rhetorical question. Lili didn't want an answer. She just wanted to get something off her chest.

"Everything always has to be the way she wants it. Like the damn cupcakes."

"Cupcakes?" Lauren asked, thoroughly lost.

"They're for the dance. For dessert. Cute, right? It was my idea. But Ashley insists we have to get them made from this recipe her chef provided." Lili dug into her bag and fished out a crumpled piece of paper. "But I can't find a baker who'll do it. They won't use a home recipe. You can either order their cupcakes or make your own. Some kind of insurance thing. And I'm not about to bake a hundred cupcakes."

"Why can't Ashley's chef do it, then?"

"Because apparently that's not her job." Lili shook her head. "At least according to Ashley. I've called twenty bakeries already. They all said no."

Lauren took the recipe from her and studied it. "It looks like it's just a recipe for vanilla cupcakes."

"Yeah. So?"

"So, why not just order the regular cupcakes? Ashley will never know, right? And what she doesn't know won't hurt her." That seemed an easy enough solution.

Lili's eyes shone. "You're right. Why didn't I think of that?"

She pulled out her cell phone. "Hi? We spoke earlier? Yeah. Can I just have a hundred of your regular vanilla cupcakes? Hold on, I got another call. Oh wait, don't worry, it's just a friend of mine. I'll let it go to voice mail. Yeah. Buttercream frosting. For next Friday. Yes. Delivery. You have the address already."

"Thanks, Lauren," Lili said, putting away her phone.

"No problem."

"Are you getting any T-shirts?" asked Lili, holding up her selection of sherbet-colored shirts.

Lauren was about to shake her head. Then she stopped. Lili was looking at her as if she were insane to pass up the chance to buy the shirts. And right now, she needed Lili to like her. Lauren decided to buy *one* shirt.

They did a little more shopping, until Lili noticed it had been a full half hour that she'd been separated from her two friends. But you'd think it was years the way Lili kept dialing and texting them every second. Independence was a costly experience, it seemed. Finally Lili decided to see if the twosome were still in the shoe store, and she dragged Lauren back to where they had left them. Lauren wished they'd been able to hang out, just the two of them, a little longer. Lili wasn't half as snotty as she was when the other Ashleys were around.

"There you guys are!" Lili said, dashing inside the shoe store, relief evident in her voice. Lauren saw Ashley and A. A.— she reminded herself she was one of them now and allowed to use the nicknames—seated on a velvet couch, several open shoe boxes scattered in front of them. "Oooh, cute shoes," said Lili, pouncing on the red patent-leather booties they were each holding.

"Here," A. A. said. "For you." She handed Lili one of the boxes. "Happy belated birthday. I bought Ashley a pair too, for her birthday. And one for me."

"What are they?" Lili asked, opening the box. She squealed when she saw what was inside and took a seat next to Ashley on the couch. She couldn't kick off her shoes fast enough and removed an identical pair of red boots from the lavender tissue. Lauren took a seat on the very edge of the couch. "Could you guys move?" she asked, but no one did.

"A. A.! You're a superstar!" Lili gushed, zipping up her new boots.

"Daphne just got them," Ashley said casually.

"She was here?" Lili gasped.

Ashley nodded. "She hung out with us. We're total BFFs now," she said smugly.

"Aw," Lili groaned. "What did she look like? What else did she buy?"

They don't even realize I'm here, Lauren thought, inching nearer to Lili in an attempt to take up more space since she was perched precariously on the edge, crouched in a half-sitting, half-squatting position. "Maybe I'll get a pair too," she mumbled to herself.

"Could I get this in a size five and a half?" Lauren asked a salesgirl, motioning to the shoes. Then she turned to the Ashleys, who were now all wearing their new boots. "Do you guys know what you're wearing to the dance yet?"

"God, no," A. A. replied, crossing her arms. "I don't plan that far in advance." She shrugged.

Lauren noted that the dance was that Friday. But someone like A. A., who'd always been beautiful, probably never had to worry about what she would look like. Unlike Lauren, who still did a double take whenever she saw her reflection in the mirror, since she couldn't quite believe it was her.

"Something from my mom's closet, most likely," A. A. said, fluffing her bangs. "Designers still send her great stuff all the time."

"I don't know yet either," Ashley put in.

Lili was silent, Lauren noticed.

The salesgirl returned.

"I'm sorry, those were the last size five and a half," she said, pointing to the box Ashley was holding.

"Oh, well. I guess I'll just have to order them from another store," Lauren said nonchalantly, trying not to show her distress about having been left out again. "Lili and I bought the same T-shirt," she said, in an effort to bring up the camaraderie they'd shared just a little while ago. It was just one T-shirt. And her dad could afford it.

"It's just a basic," said Lili quickly. "I mean, anyone can buy a white T-shirt, right?"

Lauren tried not to feel dissed as she looked down at her wedge boots. They pinched her feet, and she could feel a blister forming on her big toe. The Ashleys always carried off wearing high heels with an effortless grace. Did any of them ever suffer to be beautiful? The three of them were standing in front of the full-length mirror. Then they started doing high kicks together, linking arms and singing "New York, New York."

Watching Lili pull on A. A.'s pigtails and Ashley make bunny ears behind her two friends, as they laughed and pushed each other, Lauren forgot all about sabotaging their clique. All she wanted right then, more than anything in the world, was to be one of them.

24

A STAR IN NEED

"I'M HUNGRY," A. A. ANNOUNCED AS THE FOUR of them left the shoe store. She checked her watch. It seemed like it had been hours since they'd gotten off the plane, and really, all they'd eaten that day couldn't constitute a real meal.

"There's a restaurant down here that's pretty good," Lauren suggested meekly.

"Let's go," urged A. A., before Ashley and Lili could disagree. They followed Lauren to a pretty little cottage tucked in the middle of the street. As with the earlier store, there was a mob scene in front of the place, with a ceaseless stream of expensive automobiles pulling up to the sidewalk, an army of photographers staked out on either side of the entrance, and a rash of curious onlookers milling around with the restaurant's bona fide clientele. These seemed to include a large number of people hiding behind hats, caps, and sunglasses, which could only indicate major celebrity presence.

"Check out the hotties!" A. A. said, marveling at the brilliant smiles of several incredibly good-looking guys all dressed in neat blue button-down shirts, pressed khakis, and rakish striped neckties. A group of them were standing in front of a white picket fence. "Is a prep school nearby?"

"Um, they're valets," Lauren explained. "This is the Ivy."

"Oh. Nice!" A. A. smiled. She'd heard of the Ivy, of course, but had never been and instantly felt cheerful. Not just because of the celeb factor—she'd heard the food at the Ivy was pretty good, at least it should be better than the New Age tofu joints her mother always dragged her to every time they were in Los Angeles.

Lauren walked straight to the front of the line, and A. A. noted how she was greeted warmly by the maître d'. That girl sure had changed. Last year Lauren was so shy she could barely even speak up when the teachers called on her in class. Now she was maneuvering through a crowded Hollywood restaurant like she owned it. Not to mention that she knew Billy Reddy, and her driver might just be laxjock. It was like some geek-to-goddess story. A. A. wondered where Dex had gone for the afternoon. She was disappointed that he hadn't hung around. But maybe it was for the best, since today was all about girl-bonding.

The maître d' led them to a sun-dappled table in the

front patio, and several diners at the adjoining table looked up to see who they were. A. A. hoped they weren't too disappointed when they saw that the girls were nobody, although from the way Ashley and Lili were walking, you'd think they were People's Choice Award winners.

"My dad took us here for lunch last time," Lauren said, opening a leather-bound menu. "Try the Cobb salad, it's fantastic." At that moment their waiter, easily the most handsome guy A. A. had seen in the last few minutes, appeared to take their order.

"Four Cobb salads?" he asked. "Let me guess, dressing on the side?"

The four of them nodded. A. A. figured they were all too dazzled by his beauty to speak.

"Is it just me? Or are the regular people in L.A. a lot more good-looking than the regular people anywhere else?" Lili asked.

"Everyone's prettier here," agreed Lauren. "Maybe it's in the water."

"Totally." Ashley nodded. "This is where we belong."

"Maybe we should move here," A. A. said, taking a sip of her iced tea. "For the valets alone." She looked around the restaurant, enjoying the warmth of the day and experiencing a pleasant buzz from being near so many famous and beautiful people. She was about to take another sip from her glass when she felt a sharp kick from underneath the table. Lili jumped too, upsetting her glass of lemonade. Ashley, of course.

"What?" asked A. A., a bit irritated now that her shin was throbbing. Ashley had been so weird all day, especially about shopping. She was usually unstoppable, but all she'd bought today was some ridiculous plastic cup. She was glad she'd bought Ashley and Lili the shoes. Her mother never even checked the bills—she just forwarded them straight to her ex-husband's secretary. A. A.'s clothing allowance was funded by child support.

She followed Ashley's eyes and saw a lanky, towheaded guy walking toward them. Only a movie star as famous as Rake Parkins could get away with wearing a T-shirt that read "Just Another Rich Kid," along with jeans that were so holey they dragged on the floor. He was wildly and excessively handsome to the point of being almost too pretty.

Lili's eyes grew wide, and A. A. giggled behind her drink.

Rake stopped right at their table and, to A. A.'s growing amazement, said hello to Lauren. She introduced them one by one, but they were so starstruck that even Ashley couldn't manage more than a mumbled "Hello."

"How. Do. You. Know. Rake. Parkins. Question mark," Ashley demanded when Rake left.

"My dad invested in his new movie. He came over to our house a couple of times over the summer. He's really sweet, and he and his girlfriend have the cutest baby," Lauren said, taking a warm roll from the bread basket and buttering it heavily. She acted as if it were a fact of life that her social life revolved around movie stars.

Then she giggled, and A. A. began to truly like her for the first time. "You know, when I first met Rake I almost peed in my pants," Lauren admitted. "But after a couple of days of having him as a houseguest, I realized he's just a normal guy. He was so messy. He would leave wet towels and half-empty cups of coffee everywhere. And he expected everyone to pick up after him."

"Omigod, I'd totally take one of Rake's wet towels," Ashley offered.

"Me too," added Lili. Lili's name should be Me Too instead of Lili, A. A. thought.

The too-handsome-to-be-just-a-waiter waiter returned with their salads. The girls dug in, and A. A. noticed that Ashley was picking at hers like she always did, inspecting it from every angle, turning over every piece of spring lettuce and crumbled blue cheese as methodically as a CSI investigator brushing carpet fibers.

"Is something wrong with your food?" Lauren asked, looking concerned.

"No," said Ashley sharply, exchanging a meaningful glance with A. A.

"Ashley always does this, don't worry," A. A. told Lauren as Ashley cleared her throat, called the waiter over, and whispered something to him that only A. A. could hear.

"No, ma'am," the waiter said, shaking his head.

"You're sure?" Ashley asked.

"Yes, ma'am."

Ashley eyed the waiter and looked at the salad suspiciously, and only after a long time did she begin to eat.

A. A. was about to ask Lauren if any other movie stars had stayed in her house when Lili's phone rang. "Oh, hi, Tommy," Lili said, in her most professional tone of voice. She gave the other girls a thumbs-up. "Yes. It's Friday night. Don't forget, okay? Fri-day night. The fifth day of the week. I gave you the address yesterday. Don't tell me you already lost it? Okay, I'll give it to you again."

"DJ Tommy?" asked A. A., once Lili had gotten off the phone.

"Who's DJ Tommy?" Lauren wanted to know.

"He's only, like, the best DJ in the city, hello," Ashley said.

"Except he's supremely flaky. He did my brother's friend's bar mitzvah and showed up so late the party was almost over," A. A. reminded them.

"Lil, make sure he gets there on time," said Ashley.

"Don't worry, I'm on it. I told him the dance starts at two."

A. A. knew Lili would get it done. Nothing seemed to be impossible with Lili and her Blackberry. She could probably plan the takeover of a small country with that thing.

They were done with their salads and had moved on to the fruit cobbler (four spoons) when a familiar blonde crashed into their table.

"I hope you guys don't mind," Daphne Shepard said breathlessly. "But the pap patrol is out there and I don't want them to see me with Rake." She waved at Rake Parkins across the patio. "Is it okay if I leave the restaurant with you?"

Was it okay?

First off, Daphne was now dating Rake? What happened to the model girlfriend and the baby? Major inside information! Secondly, they had to pretend to be her posse? Could that be any more awesome? This was so much better than reading *US Weekly*. They were living it.

"But here's the thing," Daphne said. "My driver's stuck in traffic, and I told Rake I'd meet him at the Mondrian in five minutes. I wouldn't ask, but . . ."

"We have a car," Lauren assured her.

"Why don't we have Dex pull up right in front of the restaurant and make sure the car's running when we all get in?" A. A. suggested smoothly. "And then we can just drop you off at the hotel." This was just like when her mom had to dodge the scandal sheets when she was caught leaving the lipo clinic last year. Her mom had taught her all about how to make an effective exit when photographers were involved. Keep moving with your head down, and never look directly at the camera. She looked at Lauren. "Where is Dex?"

"He's parked right across the street," said Lauren. "You think he'd let a valet drive that car? Let me tell him the plan."

A few minutes later, all four girls surrounded Daphne as they exited the restaurant to a torrent of flashbulbs, hotfooting it to the Cadillac, where Dex had put up the roof for extra security. After making sure everyone was inside, A. A. slammed the door behind her. "Go, go, go!" she yelled to Dex, who winked at her from the driver's seat.

A. A. smiled at Daphne, who was already on the phone with her clandestine boyfriend. She marveled that it was true what they said—in Hollywood stars really fell out of the sky, or in their case, on your dessert.

25

AT A SLEEPOVER PARTY, WHO SAID ANYTHING ABOUT SLEEP?

I T WAS ALREADY DARK WHEN THEY ARRIVED back in San Francisco, and Lili was exhausted, but it was a good exhausted, the kind that came from spending a great day with your friends blowing through way too much money, eating way too many things that were bad for you, and knowing you would do it all again if you could. The four girls were zombies on the flight back to the city, but when they arrived at the Pages' mansion in the marina, Lili could feel their energy return.

Lili loved sleepover parties, especially since her parents never let her throw them because they were too worried her friends would be too loud and wake up her baby sisters. A. A. sometimes had them over, and they'd spy on A. A.'s brother and his friends and order room service all night, but mostly they had sleepovers at Ashley's house, because they *always* hung out at Ashley's house.

Even for Lili's twelfth birthday, she had to get ready for her party at Ashley's house instead of her own, because Ashley wanted to "surprise" her with a gift before the party. The gift turned out to be a framed photograph of Ashley. Lili kept it in a drawer in her bathroom next to the toilet. Just for once Lili would love to get ready at her own house instead of having to drag all her makeup and her ceramic flat iron (which weighed a ton) to Ashley's.

Okay, so maybe her mom could be a little strict. Maybe hanging out at her house wouldn't be as fun anyway, since they weren't allowed to watch anything but PBS, and they had to use the computer in the kitchen only.

She followed as Lauren led the way to her bedroom, which was two stories. Upstairs was a loft sleep-and-play area with shelves of books, dozens of toys, a computer cubby, and four built-in bunk beds that had flat-screen televisions installed at the foot of each bed. Downstairs Lili saw a king-size bed, a vanity with theater lighting and a plush cushioned seat, and mirrored closets that took up the whole back wall. It was lavish and extravagant, but she expected nothing less after seeing Air Force Page.

"You can put your stuff in here," Lauren told them, indicating an empty closet near the bathroom. "I'm changing into pj's," she added, disappearing into a bathroom.

Lili wondered why Lauren wouldn't change outside with the rest of them as the three slipped into their matching pajamas: pink glitter tanks with "The Ashleys" monogrammed in front and striped cotton capri pants from Limited Too, her hands-down favorite store at the mall. Sure, Robertson Boulevard was great and all, but the local Galleria was just as good in a pinch. And you didn't need a private jet to get there.

Lauren came out of the bathroom wearing a sloppy old oversize T-shirt that said "Cal" (for UC Berkeley) and faded sweatpants. She stared at the Ashleys in their glitter pj's. Lili couldn't help but feel a little sorry for the girl. Didn't she know that everything had a style quotient? In any event, Lauren had just failed the sleepwear category. "You guys want to play a board game?" Lauren asked.

"Sure—Scruples?" suggested A. A.

"Or What If?" Lili said.

"Nah, let's play Seven Deadly Sins," Ashley decided.

They all looked at Lauren hopefully, but she just stood there in her bunny slippers, looking distressed. "I don't have any of those," she told them. She opened a closet and removed boxes of Monopoly, Sorry, Clue, Cranium, and Trivial Pursuit. They were all brand-new and still wrapped in plastic. Lili guessed correctly that Lauren's mom had purchased them especially for her first sleepover party.

Ashley crinkled her nose, a dangerous sign. "No, thanks," she said politely, although it was obvious that she thought Lauren was a bit of a dweeb for imagining they would be interested in playing any of those games.

"We could make ice-cream sundaes," Lauren said, a bit desperately. "Or s'mores. We could build a campfire outside."

A. A. yawned without covering her mouth. "I'm sleepy," she said drowsily, lying down on the silk comforter on top of Lauren's bed.

"Don't be a tool, it's not that late," said Ashley, sitting next to A. A. and giving her a friendly shove. "It's not even close to midnight."

"What about giving each other makeovers?" Lauren asked frantically. "I just got a ton of new stuff from Sephora." She lugged a train case full of cosmetics out of the bathroom and spilled it all over the duvet.

"Can I have this?" Ashley asked, plucking a Chanel lip gloss from the pile. She pocketed it without awaiting an answer.

Makeovers were so sixth grade. Poor Lauren, Lili thought. She had absolutely no idea how to throw the perfect sleepover party. Really, it was so easy.

"You guys, you know what we could do," Lili said, knowing it was time to save the evening, since Ashley looked content to watch Lauren squirm and A. A. could barely keep her eyes open. She pulled out the Gregory Hall directory she kept in her bag. A. A. had nicked it from her brother's room last year, and they took turns hiding it for safekeeping. The front of the book was all faded and torn, and there were chai and water stains on some of the pages. It had survived many a sleepover party.

"What's that?" asked Lauren, as she stacked the board games back in the closet and several stuffed animals tumbled out and hit her in the face.

"You'll see," Lili said, sitting next to Ashley on the bed and riffling through the pages. She nudged Ashley. "Do you think we should start with . . ." She let the sentence trail off, since she knew Ashley knew what she was thinking. They had talked about it while Lauren was in the bathroom.

Ashley looked at Lauren and raised an eyebrow. "Yeah."

"Whose phone are we using?" A. A. asked, rubbing her eyes and looking a lot more awake now that something interesting was happening. She pushed herself up on her elbows.

"Give it here," said Ashley, taking the phone book out of Lili's hands. She always had to run the show. "Where's your phone?" she demanded.

Lauren hunted down the cordless and brought it over. The four of them huddled close to one another as Ashley continued to flip through the pages of the directory.

"Do you think he'll be home?" Lili asked, nervously twisting a lock of her hair. This was her favorite part of any sleepover, but it was the most nerve-wracking, too. She felt her stomach drop at what they were about to do. Even though she wasn't going to be the one doing the deed, she felt terrified for Lauren. It was scary to find out exactly how you rated.

"We can only hope," Ashley said, leafing through the Rs— Ramsey, Reading, Reckler—until she found the one they were looking for.

"What's going on?" Lauren asked, trying to look over Ashley's shoulder.

"Should we tell her?" said Ashley.

"Tell me what?"

"Do it," Lili urged. Put the poor girl out of her misery. Besides, they had to do it now before it got too late in the evening.

Ashley deposited the phone book in Lauren's lap. It was open to Billy Reddy's page. There was a photo of Billy, looking tousled and gorgeous, along with his address and phone number.

"What do you want me to do this with this?" Lauren asked.

"Billy Reddy's your friend, right?" asked Ashley. "You keep telling us how close you guys are."

"Uh-huh." Lauren fidgeted, and the color drained from her cheeks. Lili had the distinct feeling that Lauren's vaunted connection to Billy wasn't as strong as she kept implying.

"Okay, then. He should be able to accept a rank call from you," Ashley said.

"What's a rank call?" asked Lauren, as A. A. punched in a series of numbers on the telephone.

"It's ringing!" Lili whispered, feeling so excited she wanted to puke.

"You're about to find out," Ashley said, handing Lauren the phone. "Now, when he picks up the phone, this is what you say. . . ."

26

CALLING YOUR CRUSH:
TEN CENTS A MINUTE.
HAVING HIM ACTUALLY PICK
UP THE PHONE: PRICELESS.

"HELLO?" A DEEP VOICE ASKED.

"Hey, is this Billy?" Lauren asked, keeping her voice as light and casual as she could possibly make it.

"Uh-huh."

"Hey, it's Lauren. Um . . ." She stalled. Did they really expect her to do this? She looked at their expectant faces. Yes. They did. The Ashleys were hanging on every word. What if he had no idea who she was? Should she remind him? "I'm planning to come to your lacrosse game next week with some friends," she said hurriedly, hoping it would jog his memory. "Dex says you guys just need one more game to make it to the play-offs."

"Oh, yeah. Hey, Lauren. Good to hear from you. Does Dex need to talk to me or something?" Billy asked, sounding a little more awake.

"Ask him! Do it!" Ashley whispered fiercely, while Lili and A. A. looked like they were going to keel over with excitement.

Lauren gulped. She would have to do what they told her if she wanted to salvage this sleepover. So far, neither her ideas nor her mom's had been met with any level of enthusiasm—she hoped Trudy wouldn't notice that none of the board games had been opened. If she wanted the girls to like her—and after spending the day with them, she really wanted them to, even if she planned to . . . what did she plan to do again? She gripped the phone more tightly.

"No . . . no . . . this isn't about Dex. Um. Billy?"

"Still here," replied Billy.

"Will you accept a rank call?" she asked, her stomach twisted in knots. She had no idea what she had just asked him and fully expected him to slam the phone down immediately.

But to her immense surprise, he only groaned. "Oh no, not one of these again."

"I'm sorry," she said, completely flabbergasted that he even knew what she was talking about. "This was totally not my idea, trust me." She saw Ashley's face falter and felt a little more empowered.

"No . . . no problem. I'll do it. I don't want you to get penalized. What do you want me to rank?"

"What do I want you to rank?" Lauren repeated, looking at the girls for help.

"Put him on speaker!" ordered Ashley. From the way the Ashleys suddenly exploded in a flurry of activity, it was obvious they hadn't thought Billy would play along either. "C'mon, we have to hear this!"

But Lauren waved her away, not wanting to share Billy with them just yet. *What do I do?* she mouthed, as Lili shoved a piece of paper toward her with a list of attributes written on it, while A. A. handed her a pen.

She looked down and began reading from it. "Um. Hair?"

"Nine," he said.

She wrote "9" on the paper and noticed the reaction on the Ashleys' faces when she did so. Ashley looked like she'd just been stabbed in the heart.

"Smile?" she asked next, as it dawned on her that a "rank call" was like some sort of beauty contest, where a girl called a boy so that the boy could judge her on a scale of one to ten in a number of categories. It was sick, twisted, and totally awesome. Billy seemed to take it really seriously, too. She could tell he was thinking through every category. Weighing her.

Deciding how attractive she was and then putting a number on it. Her mother had always told her that beauty contests were horrible examples of patriarchal oppression and that true beauty came from within, but she didn't know the Ashleys.

"Smile? I'll have to give it a nine as well," Billy said.

When she wrote down "9" for smile, Lili shook her so vigorously in congratulations that Lauren almost dropped the phone.

Lauren felt her confidence grow as she went down the list, including "personality," "clothes," and "intellect." So far she was batting a decent average. "Last one," she said. "Body?"

There was a moment of silence on the other end, and then "Six," came the not-so-exciting reply.

"Oh." That was her lowest score so far. She tried not to feel too insulted. "Okay, I guess that's it. Thanks, Billy. Good luck on your lacrosse game next week." She hung up the phone, her palms still sweaty from the conversation.

"I can't believe Billy Reddy just ranked you!" A. A. crowed, grabbing the paper from Lauren's hand.

"You're so lucky!" said Lili, her cheeks bright red. "None of us has ever been ranked by Billy Reddy."

"That's because he probably doesn't know who we are," A. A. said mildly.

"A. A., shut up," said Ashley. She took the paper and

made a few quick calculations with her pen, her forehead scrunching in concentration. Lauren assumed it was because math was Ashley's worst subject.

"You averaged an eighty-eight, not a seventy-eight," A. A. said, correcting her friend's addition as she looked over Ashley's shoulder. "Not bad for your first rank."

"But he gave me a six for body?" said Lauren, twisting her mouth. "It's probably because I'm really flat, right?" She pulled on the collar of her T-shirt and looked down. Sadly, they hadn't grown in the last five minutes. Her mother had made her wear a training bra, although she wasn't sure exactly what the bra was training her chest to do. Grow?

"Do guys really like girls with bigger boobs?" mused Lili, who was similarly handicapped in that area. "My sisters said big boobs are a total nightmare, and it's so much better to be flat."

"Keep telling yourself that, Lil, maybe one day you'll believe it," Ashley teased, throwing a pillow at her.

"Okay, so what do I do now?" asked Lauren, finally feeling able to relax in their company. She'd pulled off her first rank call, with Billy Reddy, no less! Later she'd have to remember every aspect of their conversation so she could savor it all over again.

"You pass the phone to someone else, and they have to call a boy of your choosing," Lili explained, plumping the pillow Ashley had thrown at her and stuffing it underneath her head.

"Who should I pass it to?"

"Anyone you want," Ashley said, a bit impatiently.

"Pass it to A. A.," suggested Lili.

Lauren obligingly passed the cordless and A. A. straightened up, took the pad and pencil, and affected a brisk, no-nonsense demeanor. "Who's the lucky victim?" she asked.

"Tri Fitzpatrick," Ashley prodded, poking Lauren in the side.

"Okay. Tri Fitzpatrick," Lauren obliged.

A. A. turned as pink as her tank top. "I can't ask Tri for a rank call! He's my friend," she said, looking almost panicked.

"Which is why you should have him rank you," Ashley said in a reasonable tone. "Don't you want to know what he really thinks?"

"NO!" A. A. shook her head.

"Too bad," Ashley said. "You have to do it. You know what happens if you forfeit." She smiled that evil Ashley Spencer smile that Lauren had seen directed her way a thousand times in the refectory, accompanied by mocking laughter.

"For the last time, Ashley, I am not going to streak a Gregory Hall lacrosse game if I forfeit a rank call. It's just not going to happen," A. A. huffed.

"Whatever. Lame-o," said Ashley, making a circling motion next to her head to indicate "crazy."

"Billy is Lauren's friend and he ranked her," Lili pointed out. "C'mon, it'll be fun. Tri's ranked all of us except you, you know."

"You don't have to do it," Lauren said, feeling bad that she'd unwittingly stumbled into another one of Ashley's power moves.

A. A. sighed. "No, I'll do it," she said roughly, picking up the phone and dialing a number. "This game is so dumb."

"And yet so addictive at the same time," said Lili wisely.

"Maybe if I'm lucky he won't be home," A. A. said, looking at her watch as the phone started to ring.

Lauren hoped so too, for A. A.'s sake. She didn't know Tri. He was one of the popular seventh-grade boys who was always hanging out with the Ashleys. He was really cute, but incredibly short.

"Put him on speaker," Ashley ordered, and A. A. reluctantly complied, hitting the button and placing the phone in the middle of their huddle.

"Domino's," a youthful voice answered.

"Ha-ha," A. A. said, leaning forward and amplifying her voice so that he would be able to hear her better. "I know it's you, The Third."

"Hey, Double-A. What's up? Am I on speaker? What's going on?"

A. A. sighed. She looked at her friends. *Do I really have to?* she mouthed.

Ashley and Lili nodded vigorously while Lauren shrugged, feeling guilty for making A. A. do something she obviously didn't want to do.

"Tri, will you accept a rank call?"

27

WERE HARRY AND SALLY RIGHT?

HERE WAS SILENCE ON THE LINE FOR A BIT, and A. A. heard nothing but the sound of, what else, a video game in the background—the rat-a-tat of an automatic weapon, the shrill cries of decapitated zombies. Then Tri came back on the line. He sounded hesitant. "From you? You want me to rank . . . you?"

"Yes, from me," A. A. said. "Just do it, okay?"

"Okay," said Tri, still sounding uncertain. "Hit me."

A. A. looked down the list. Maybe she should start with an easy one. "Personality?" she asked.

"I dunno," Tri said.

"You've accepted the call, Tri," Ashley butted in, elbowing A. A. aside for now. "You know the rules."

"Who's there?" Tri asked sharply.

"Everyone—me, Ash, Lil, Lauren," A. A. told him. "The usual."

"Personality . . . uh . . . I give you a ten," said Tri.

A. A. noticed Ashley raise her eyebrows, but a ten for personality wasn't such a surprise, considering that she and Tri were best friends. Of course he would think she had a good personality. Okay, next one.

"Hair?" she asked. God, this was truly moronic. How could she ask Tri—the guy who once showed her how to stick a noodle in her nose and make it come out her mouth—what he thought of her hair? Did he even think of her hair? She pulled on her pigtails anxiously.

"Okay. Hair. Uh. I dunno. . . ."

A. A. wished he would spit out a number, any number, just to get this thing over with. He didn't have to take it so seriously—except that was the thing. No one ever joked around with the rank calls. That was what made them so special. It was like getting a little sneak peek into a boy's mind, and somehow they had convinced the boys this was a good thing to do. A. A. was convinced that Ashley had come up with the game so she could lord it over everyone how all the boys at Gregory Hall were in love with her. Ashley was the rank call queen.

"Hair," Tri repeated. He clucked his tongue. "Ten?"

Was he serious? A. A. wrote down "10" and kicked Lili on the ankle for snickering. Lili and Ashley had teased her about Tri forever, and this was so not helping.

In the end, Tri gave her the highest rank yet in the history of rank calls: a perfect one hundred. Not even Ashley had merited that from Jonathan Tessin, the Gregory Hall eighth grader who had such a huge crush on her he used to send her slobbery IMs every day until she had to change her online handle.

A. A. didn't know what to make of it. She knew he had to be sincere, since Ashley and Lili had called Tri for their rank calls last year and he'd given Ashley a "4" for personality, while Lili had merited a "10" for intelligence—which meant he was being sincere, since she knew Tri thought Ashley was a nightmare and that Lili was really smart.

"Wow. One hundred. I don't think that's allowed. Nobody's that perfect," Lili teased. "He must be really into you."

"He's my friend," A. A. emphasized. If she had to rank Tri, she'd probably give him the same score, not that she would ever get the chance, since the girls never ranked the boys—the calls only went one way. Although she'd have to take a few points off for height, if she was being totally honest.

"Girls can't be friends with boys, everyone knows that," Ashley said. Ever since she had made them watch some old movie that was her mom's favorite, Ashley had taken to quoting from it as if it were a manual on modern dating. Which was silly, since everyone knew that movie was from, like, the Dark Ages.

"Ashley, that is so stupid," said A. A., but she kept hearing Tri's low voice—when did it get that low? Had she never noticed before?—amplified on the speakerphone and wondered if Ashley could possibly be right.

Did Tri like her? Did he want to be more than friends? She thought back to the last time they'd hung out. He'd come over the other week so they could watch the *Battlestar Galactica* marathon together. Then she'd beat him on the Wii as usual, and then he left. He had acted exactly the same way he always did. He certainly didn't act like he was in love with her or anything ridiculous like that.

She wondered what laxjock would think if she told him about Tri. Would he be jealous? He seemed too cool to be jealous. And besides, Tri was just her childhood friend. Laxjock was older, wiser, hotter. Dex's image came to mind.

A. A. pulled her legs up and rested her chin on her knees, curling into a ball. Next to her, Lili was getting ranked by a guy from St. Aloysius, Ashley was trying on her new Chanel lip gloss, and Lauren was passing around mugs of hot chocolate her housekeeper had just brought up to the room.

She took a sip of the dark, rich drink. It was made the way A. A. liked it—not too sweet, with only a dollop of whipped cream on top instead of a melted marshmallow. Tri always made the hot chocolate when they hung out at his place, since A. A. tended to burn it. Cooking was not one of her strong points. He always remembered to add the whipped cream.

A. A. imagined the two of them as a couple, holding hands when they walked down Union Street, Tri waiting for her in front of Miss Gamble's, the two of them meeting for coffee. Tri *kissing* her. His handsome face leaning in toward hers, his eyes closing—he did have the longest, darkest lashes she'd ever seen on a boy, she had noticed once when he fell asleep on their couch watching television—and pictured their lips touching over a steaming mug of hot chocolate.

She made a face. She could sooner imagine Tri beating her at Resident Evil.

28

THESE GIRLS ARE TWELVE GOING ON TWENTY-FIVE

"I'M TIRED," ASHLEY SAID, WHICH WAS HER cue to let everyone know the sleepover party was over. It was almost three o'clock in the morning and they'd tried on all of Lauren's clothes, a remarkable amount of which had never been worn and had dangling price tags to prove it. And they'd danced around the room trying out some new Pants-Off Dance-Off moves, and rank-called half the guys in the Gregory Hall directory.

All in all, a good weekend, Ashley thought as the four of them made their way to the top floor of Lauren's room and settled in their bunks for the evening. Lauren had a sweet setup; this was way better than sleeping bags. Why hadn't she ever thought of that?

Ashley chose the top bunk. The sheets were so crisp and

they opened with an audible crack like they did at the Ritz in Paris. She slipped underneath the lavender-smelling goose-down comforter. Then her stomach grumbled, and she felt a sharp pain in the lower half of her belly. Had she eaten something bad? But this was more than a stomachache. She felt something weird. Something icky. Oh, no. Not here. She jumped up and quickly climbed down from the top bunk, ran down the spiral stairs, and locked herself in Lauren's bathroom. She checked. Yep. Her "little friend" had chosen that moment to arrive.

Lauren's bathroom was a vast space, with a freestanding antique claw tub, a shower stall big enough for three people, and a row of closets. Ashley began opening drawers and closet doors, searching madly. She found stacks of plush towels, hand lotions in every fragrance, dozens of tissue boxes, and cartons of mouthwash and floss, but not one single pad.

Ashley sat on the toilet, thinking. Sure, she could ask Lili or A. A. if they had any, but she didn't feel like announcing it to everyone just then. How could Lauren not have gotten her period yet? As far as Ashley knew, she was the last one in the class. And she had been more than happy to wait. This sucked.

There was a soft knock on the door. She opened it a crack and saw Lauren standing there in those pathetic bunny slippers and that faded old T-shirt. She looked like she was twelve. Okay, so they were twelve, but still, hello.

"What?"

"I need to use the bathroom to take out my contacts."

"Aren't there, like, eight bathrooms in this house?"

Lauren looked at her. "You don't look good. Do you feel okay?"

"I just got my period, like, for the first time," Ashley snapped. Oh, well. She had to tell somebody, or else bleed all over everything. "Do you have a pad or something?"

In answer, Lauren walked into the bathroom and opened a drawer hidden behind the towel rack. She handed Ashley a small pink square.

"Oh. Em. Gee. Lifesaver. Thanks," said Ashley, snatching it quickly.

Lauren kept staring at her. "Do I have something on my face?" Ashley asked.

"No." Lauren shook her head.

Ashley closed the door firmly. She'd never understand that girl. But she was glad Lauren hadn't made a big deal out of it. She was cool. And she'd pulled off that rank call with Billy Reddy, too. Ashley felt better knowing Billy had given Lauren a six for body. Everyone knew the "body" question was the most revealing one and showed whether a boy actually liked you or not. Billy obviously just thought of Lauren as a friend. She'd have to ask Lauren if they could hang out with Billy after the lacrosse game next week. Maybe they could all come back to Ashley's house for snacks. Her chef made the best no-carb brownies.

When she returned to the room, the other girls were all watching different shows on their individual flat-screens.

"You guys, don't be so antisocial," she chided. "Turn off the TVs. Let's play Castles in the Air instead. I'll start." She looked up at the ceiling, charmed by the seascape mural someone had painted on it. "My castle is a classic six co-op in Manhattan, with a view of Central Park. I'm going to grow up to chair benefit committees and get my picture taken in *Vogue*. Marc Jacobs is going to be my best friend."

"You always say that," A. A. said sleepily from the bottom bunk.

"So what? What's yours, then?"

"My castle is a beach house in Malibu right on the cliffs, and me and my gorgeous husband, laxjock—if he doesn't turn out to be a fat, homeschooled loser—are going to live there with our four dogs," said A. A.

"Mmm." Ashley sighed happily. She loved this game and couldn't wait to grow up. She forced her friends to play it all the time. It was the best way to drift off to sleep, dreaming about what the future held. "Lil?"

"You guys already know what mine is," Lili said with a yawn from the top of the other bunk.

"The same as Ashley's," called A. A.

Lili didn't deny it.

Ashley snorted. "You're so predictable, Lil. Good night, girls."

"Wait!" A. A. protested. "Lauren hasn't told us what her Castle is."

"Oh, I don't have one," Lauren said meekly.

"Everyone has a dream, Lauren," Ashley reprimanded. "C'mon, tell us what you want your house to be like when you grow up."

Lauren tossed and turned in the bottom bunk. Finally she spoke. "My castle is a tiny cottage in the woods. Something small and wonderful and perfectly cozy. There's a garden in the back, with the most beautiful flowers, and a library filled with all my favorite books." She held her breath.

"Do the seven dwarves live there?" teased Lili.

"Or Grandma and the big bad wolf?" A. A. laughed, but her voice was warm.

Ashley could picture Lauren's tiny little cottage. It seemed weird to want something so small, but it sounded pleasant enough. Maybe some people didn't like to dream big. To each her own. Not everyone could be an Ashley Spencer, hello. Not even Lili, even though she wanted it bad enough, anyone could see that.

"I think it sounds nice," Ashley murmured. "I like it."

29

WAKING UP ON THE WRONG SIDE OF BED

HEN LAUREN WOKE UP THE NEXT morning, she felt a rush of warm water on her skin, and she jerked awake with a start. Her hand was immersed in a bowl of warm water and her sheets were damp. What was this? She pulled out her hand and looked at it dumbly, shaking droplets all over the floor. She blinked, looking around the room. Everything looked fuzzy without her contacts, and she fumbled for her glasses, which she'd placed near her pillow. They were thick glass-bottom specs with a broken black plastic frame held together by duct tape. Now that she wore contacts, she hadn't seen the need to buy new glasses and had stubbornly held on to them as a souvenir from her old life.

She put them on and the world came into focus. The

Ashleys were sitting cross-legged on the carpet across from her.

"Wake up, Sleeping Beauty," Ashley said.

"Or should we say Peeing Beauty?" asked Lili with a laugh.

Lauren felt her throat constrict, and she kicked off the comforter. Everything was wet. It was mortifying. How could this happen?

A. A. handed her a mirror. "If you break it you get seven years' bad luck," she said, and the Ashleys erupted into mad giggles.

Lauren looked in the mirror. Someone had written "I Love Pee" on her forehead in red ink.

"The girls at school are going to love hearing about this," said Lili cheerfully.

Lauren blinked, fighting an onslaught of tears. She'd never found practical jokes very funny, but this was too much. Especially after she'd gone to bed believing that the four of them could be real friends after all. Last night she'd even felt *close* to Ashley. It was so weird to see her like that—all nervous and jumpy just because she'd gotten her period. She'd never thought of Ashley as having problems before, but last night Ashley had seemed . . . insecure. Almost like a real person. She'd gone to bed thinking she had finally made three new friends.

But that obviously wasn't the case this morning.

"Maybe we should call Billy and tell him about how she's

not toilet trained yet," Ashley mocked, filing her nails with an emery board and leaving nail dust all over the carpet.

"Maybe her parents should use rubber sheets," agreed A. A.

Lili danced around, waving her cell phone. It was a photo of Lauren sleeping with her mouth open, drool coming out of the side of her lips. She tried to snatch it away, but Lili held it just out of reach. "This is so going on our blog!"

Lauren wiped the letters on her forehead, leaving an ugly red mark. Her eyes filled with hot, angry tears. This was their idea of friendship? "Screw you guys," she said bitterly. "I'll show you."

"What was that?" asked Ashley, tossing aside her nail file.

"You heard me," Lauren spat.

"Jeez, Lauren, take it easy," A. A. urged. "It's just a joke."

But Lauren was tired of being the butt of the Ashleys' jokes.

"You guys suck. You're just a bunch of losers," she said, her voice gathering speed and fervor. She felt reckless and liberated. All the resentment she'd felt at being left out and picked on all those years—she remembered the taste of mud all too well—plus all the terrible lies they spread about her even after she tried so hard to be just like them—the pig nose, the Mafia rumors.

"You're all fake and pathetic. Lili can't breathe without asking Ashley if she can. A. A.'s a boy-crazy ditz and Ashley—

you're just *so mean*. You could be a nice person, but you aren't, you choose to be the exact opposite. You're just a spoiled, rotten little monster."

There. That would show them. She took a deep breath and expected the sky to come crashing down. But the earth was still moving. She had told them exactly what she thought of them and she'd survived. But now what?

The silence in the room was deafening. The girls looked shell-shocked from Lauren's outburst. Lili looked pale, and A. A. couldn't look her in the eye.

Ashley merely stood up, hitching up her pajama bottoms. Even first thing in the morning, she was so pretty, with her blond hair just messed up enough so it looked cute. Lauren knew her hair was tangled into a bird's nest from all her tossing and turning. She felt like a dork all over again, especially with the glasses back on her face.

"Anything else you want to add?" Ashley asked mildly.

Lauren shrugged. She'd already told them the worst. But wait—why not put the final nail in the coffin? What did she have to lose? She looked Ashley directly in the eye, so that they were face-to-face. "Yes, I do. Everyone in school hates you. You don't have any real friends."

Ashley smiled without showing any of her teeth. "Funny, because I think that tomorrow it's you who won't have any friends, hello."

"Not that you had any in the first place," Lili said, shaking her head sadly.

"You guys, I think this has gone on long enough," A. A. pleaded. She looked at Lauren. "I really wish you hadn't said that."

Lauren's stomach dropped. Something in A. A.'s tone of voice made her feel a little queasy.

Then Ashley and A. A. brushed aside their bangs. Lauren felt her anger dissipate and turn into the most gut-wrenching horror. They both had "I Love Pee" on their foreheads too.

Oh, holy crap.

"The first person who wakes up always pulls a prank on everyone else. It's a sleepover party tradition," explained Ashley briskly. "Lili got up first this time. Look around. There are bowls of water on all the other bunks."

Lauren didn't have to look. She knew they would be there. She had read it completely, completely wrong. She was so off base. How could she be so smart and yet so incredibly stupid at the same time?

"And no one really pees," A. A. said. "We just put a little water on the covers so you think you did."

"Look," said Ashley, showing Lauren her cell phone. Lauren held it and looked at the screen. It showed A. A. sleeping with her mouth wide open, and someone had drawn flies all over it; another photo showed Ashley sleeping with her thumb in her mouth.

"You think you're so special? Check the freezer—you'll find A. A.'s huge bazookas and my Chantelle in there along with your sad excuse for a bra," Ashley said, as Lauren continued to study the photos.

Lauren's mind was blank. What had she done? She had thought the Ashleys were back to torturing her again, but instead, the prank was an *initiation* into their group. She was finally being treated like one of the Ashleys, and she had completely blown it!

"We're going." said Ashley coldly. "Thank God my mom is picking us up early for dance-team practice."

"Sorry to hear you don't really like us after all," A. A. said, pulling on a slouchy Gregory Hall sweatshirt over her pj's. "Maybe this is for the best."

Lili just kept shaking her head.

"Lauren? Piece of advice?" Ashley offered, gazing at her with contempt. "If I were you, I would seriously think about transferring out of Miss Gamble's. Your life there is over. It'll be worse than you ever thought. You thought kindergarten was bad? Welcome to junior high, Zero."

"Guys, I was just . . . I didn't mean it. . . ." Lauren scrambled, getting up from the floor and tripping on her socks, scraping her knee on the ground. She felt like bawling.

This was by far the worst thing that had ever happened to her. Worse than having mud shoved up her nose in kindergarten. Worse because this time, the Ashleys weren't to blame. She had no one to blame but herself.

"Save it, Lauren," Ashley said, cutting her off.

Lauren watched them pack their bags in silence and walk single file out of her bedroom. She ran over to the window and saw the girls exit the front door and climb into a tan Range Rover parked by the curb. Then the car pulled away and the Ashleys were out of her life . . . *forever.*

She held her face in her hands and felt the tears flow down her cheeks. How did this happen?

On Monday her life would be over.

30

YOU'RE NEVER FULLY DRESSED
WITHOUT A SMIRK

AUREN WASN'T AT SCHOOL ON MONDAY. SHE wasn't at school on Tuesday, either, and by Friday no one had seen or heard from her. Lili didn't want to worry, but the sight of Lauren's empty seat in every class nagged at her conscience.

"Maybe she's dead," Ashley said.

"She's not dead," A. A. snorted.

"If I were her, I would wish I were dead," declared Ashley. "Freaking out like that? She's demented!"

"You know, you didn't have to get all medieval," Lili said, cinching the belt on her trench coat a little tighter. "It *was* a pretty tough prank. She was bound to get upset."

The three of them were walking up the hill back to school on Friday afternoon. Classes had ended early so the seventh and eighth graders could get ready for the mixer, and Lili had met her friends at the corner so they could all walk into the dance together. A. A. and Ashley had gotten ready at Ashley's house, but for the first time in Ashley history, Lili had made excuses and had gotten ready at home instead.

At first it was fun to have the bathroom all to herself for once and not have to fight for space in front of the mirror or listen to that awful StripHall Queens song again, which Ashley would insist on blasting at top volume. But when she couldn't decide whether to curl her hair or to wear it up, she wished Ashley was there to tell her what looked better, and the gossiping veejays on MTV were no match for A. A.'s jokey banter.

"I'm sure she'll be back. Maybe she has the flu," A. A. speculated.

"Maybe," Ashley allowed, but Lili knew that as far as Ashley was concerned, Lauren had fallen off the face of the earth, and it was safer to stay there than to ever show her face to them again.

Where was Lauren? Would she really miss a whole week of school just because Ashley had pulled some crazy Mean Girls act? Wasn't she a grade-grind? Sure, the Ashleys would go back to snubbing her as usual—and good luck ever sitting with them at lunch again. But Lauren had survived for years as a social outcast. You'd think she'd be used to it.

"Bet she shows up at the dance," said A. A. as they arrived at the school doors and walked down the back stairs to the Little Theater, where the dance was being held. They had come early in order to make sure everything was in place, since they were in charge of the event.

"You're on. That's a bet I'll win," Ashley replied. "Ooh. Look."

A red carpet led from the elevator all the way to the auditorium doors, which were cordoned off by velvet ropes and stanchions.

"Like it?" Lili asked, unhooking the rope and letting them inside. "Ladies . . . may I present 'Social Club'!"

"Lil, this is amazing!" A. A. said, looking around at the transformed space. The Little Theater was a multi-use space in the new annex with a stage for student productions, bleacher seats for pep rallies, and a parquet floor perfect for dancing, but it was utterly unrecognizable as the boring old place where they held "MODs," Middle-of-the-Day announcements. It looked, for all intents and purposes, like a fabulous New York nightclub.

"Props times three," Ashley agreed.

"Thanks." Lili smiled. Crepe paper and balloons? Not at this school. She really had done a spectacular job, if she did say so herself. The full-length windows that ran the length of the back wall were covered with draped velvet, so even if it was midafternoon, it was dark and cool inside. The better to see the light from the ten disco balls installed in the ceiling. By the stage were several low-slung couches and tiny circular tables to approximate a cocktail lounge, and the whole place was decorated with dramatic floral arrangements artfully illuminated by incandescent lighting. A uniformed staff was setting up the fully catered buffet with seafood, prime rib, and sushi stations.

"We're getting TV coverage, too," Lili told them. "Sheridan Riley's dad is a producer at a local television station and is sending over a full camera crew, and along with the yearbook club photographers, we're going to have real paparazzi from the *San Francisco Chronicle*."

"How'd you manage that?" A. A. asked, admiring a jet-black napkin with SOCIAL CLUB monogrammed on it.

"Simple. I just pitched them a story on the 'hot under-thirteen set.' You know journalists are always looking for new trends."

"Is there a hot under-thirteen set?" A. A. asked, sounding amused.

"Yes. Us. Hello," Ashley replied, glancing around approvingly.

"Oh, I meant to tell you, we went a little over budget," Lili said sheepishly.

"Well, that's what the Mothers Committee is for." Ashley shrugged.

"You guys, I'm so nervous," said A. A., as they went back to the lockers to put away their coats.

"Today's the day, huh?" Ashley said, removing her coat and hanging it up neatly on her locker hook. "Laxjock—unmasked at last!"

"What if he doesn't like me?" A. A. agonized.

"He's going to like you, of course he's going to like you. He'd be crazy not to," Lili said, keeping her coat on just a little longer.

She glanced over to see what the two other girls were wearing. A. A. had on a sleeveless swingy trapeze dress, the kind that would make any other girl who wore it immediately look ten pounds heavier. But on A. A. it was just right—light, breezy, and effortlessly stylish. That was the thing about A. A.: She never cared about clothing and yet she always came up with the most fashionable things. Guess it helped when your mom used to be a supermodel. Ashley was wearing some kind of white dress—Lili didn't get a chance to check it out longer, since she was so nervous about what she was about to do.

"You guys ready?" Ashley asked, closing her locker door.

"Yeah," said Lili. Now or never. She took off her coat and hung it up in her locker, her cheeks crimson.

She turned around, steeling herself for whatever came next. She was wearing the slinky black jersey dress that Ashley had supposedly convinced her not to buy. "I like it," she said defensively. She squared her shoulders and threw her dark glossy hair back over her shoulders. The dress looked smashing on her, and she was not going to be intimidated into settling for something less. Not this time.

But instead of yelling at her, Ashley only shrugged. "You look pretty, Lil," was all she said.

Lili exhaled. Okay. So that wasn't too bad. Ashley didn't even seem to care. What was she so worried about? Then she took a closer look at what Ashley was wearing. It was a white chiffon dress with a tight bodice and a strap that hung over only one shoulder. It had an abbreviated miniskirt with a jagged hem. It was incredibly chic and cutting-edge looking. Plus, it was white, which neither Lili nor A. A. had thought to wear. They were both in black.

"What is that?" Lili couldn't help but ask. "Where'd you get it?"

"Oh, this old thing?" Ashley drawled. "It's from the new Kate Moss for Topshop collection. My mom felt really bad about how I didn't have any money when we went shopping last weekend, and she ordered it for me all the way from London."

"It's really cool," Lili said, not even trying to keep the envy out of her voice.

"I know," said Ashley.

Lili chanced a look in the mirror at her dress. At home it had looked so sophisticated, so daring. But now it was so boring and blah.

It was just another black dress.

"I'll lend it to you sometime if you want," Ashley offered, as if she could read Lili's mind. "We're the same size, aren't we?"

"I'd love that," Lili said, smiling back at her friend. *Never underestimate Ashley Spencer*, she told herself. She had tried many times, and Ashley always found a way to come out on top. Who could step out of her shadow when Ashley kept hogging the limelight?

But there was no time to think about it for too long. As the Ashleys walked into the Little Theater, a screech erupted from the topmost bleachers, where Carly Cohen, an excitable seventh grader, had been keeping watch since three thirty. She yelled those four sweet little words every Miss Gamble's girl had been waiting to hear all day.

"THE BOYS ARE HERE!"

31

CAN YOU BOX-STEP
TO BEAT-BOX?

"**G**ENTLY! GRACIOUSLY! GIRLS! GIRLS! Calm down!"

Ashley smiled. Miss Charm was darting around like a confused bird lost in the sea of adolescent excitement. The etiquette teacher had volunteered to be a mixer chaperone, and she and Mr. Huntley, the elderly math teacher (and the school's only male professor) looked overwhelmed by the ferocious energy of their charges. "Remember your ladylike behavior!" Miss Charm despaired.

But it was no use, Ashley knew. Carly Cohen's announcement was like a clarion call, leading to a mad frenzy as all the girls scrambled to join her at the top of the steps. They crowded around the picture window, watching intently as a stream of boys in blue blazers exited a yellow school bus and walked toward the school.

"Get down!" Ashley ordered, as the boys disappeared into the front doors. "They're going to be here in a minute!"

Almost as one, the girls clattered down the steps as Ashley instructed, their high heels making a thunderous noise that echoed around the auditorium.

Miss Charm needn't have worried, Ashley thought, as the girls settled themselves quietly on the front bleachers. Ashley took a seat near the middle, Lili and A. A. on either side of her. Like her, they kept their legs prudently crossed at the ankle, and the three were the very picture of demure femininity by the time the boys arrived.

Finally the doors to the theater opened, and the Gregory Hall boys shuffled in, still wearing their uniforms, since they had come straight from class. Ashley kept her nose in the air. Really, the boys could have made more of an effort.

The boys elbowed one another, pushing and snickering. They cast sheepish glances at the rows of seated girls and moved, en masse, to the opposite wall. Ashley gave them her most welcoming smile.

The girls stared at the boys. The boys stared at the ceiling. The girls began to whisper to one another and giggle. The boys looked longingly at the buffet tables. Ashley tapped her foot impatiently. This was so not the way she'd pictured the dance happening. She noticed there wasn't even any music.

"Where's DJ Tommy?" Ashley whispered to Lili.

"He said he'd be here. I left him tons of messages this morning to remind him," Lili said, looking worried. "His people dropped his stuff off this afternoon," she added, gesturing to the DJ station in the middle of the stage, flanked by massive six-foot-tall speakers.

"What are we going to dance to, then?" Ashley whined.

"Told you he was a flake," said A. A.

"Shut up," Lili said. "You're not helping."

Ashley watched with morbid fascination as Miss Charm made her way to the turntables. *No way.* Their etiquette teacher placed a needle on a record and the scratchy sound of a familiar Chopin waltz began to play.

The girls continued to fidget in their seats. Ashley saw some of the boys bring out handheld video games and start playing with them. How rude! This was turning out to be a total disaster. Not one boy crossed the great divide of the parquet dance floor, festively stenciled with the letters VIP in the middle, while the disco balls kept turning, refracting the light.

Ashley crossed her arms. She had gotten her hair and makeup done professionally for *this*?

At last a dark-haired boy separated from the wolf pack. Tri. Thank God. Unlike the other boys, who looked like they'd just come straight from the playground, with sweaty-looking faces and messy, dirty trousers, Tri was neat, preppie, and handsome in his crested blazer, and confidently crossed the yawning expanse of the dance-floor Sahara. He stopped in front of the Ashleys.

"Hey, Tri," the three girls chorused.

"Hey." He nodded, smiling and sitting down next to A. A., of course. "This is some dance. Great music, too. Really . . . retro."

"Shut up! I just called Tommy. He just got out of AP Biology and he's going to be here any minute," Lili promised.

A. A. looked at her watch.

"You need to be somewhere?" asked Tri.

"Yeah," she said. "I'm meeting someone."

"That online boyfriend of hers," Ashley said.

"At the fountain, right." Tri nodded sagely. "Still think it's Billy Reddy?" he asked.

"No." A. A. shook her head. "Of course not. I'm so over Billy Reddy."

"He's LWN," said Ashley.

"What?" he asked.

"Last week's news."

Tri looked pleased.

"Now she thinks he's Dex Bond," Ashley told him.

The smile faded slightly from Tri's face. "Who's Dex Bond?"

"Some dude who coaches the high school lacrosse team."
Ashley shrugged.

"He's *cuuute*," added Lili.

"Oh." Tri looked down at his suede bucks.

"I'll give it a few more minutes," A. A. said. "Then I'll go."

"Right," said Tri, standing up. "Hey, um, wanna dance?"

"Sure," A. A. said, getting off the bench. "Somebody's
got to."

"Uh, I meant Ashley," Tri said.

Ashley looked up. Tri was looking at her and not A. A.
What was going on? He looked at her expectantly. He was
serious.

"You don't mind?" Ashley asked A. A.

"Why would I mind?" A. A. laughed, sitting back down,
although her cheeks had suddenly turned bright red. "Go
ahead."

"C'mon," Tri said, holding out his hand. Ashley gave him
her most charming smile. She basked in the knowledge that she
was the first girl to be asked to dance at the school's first mixer.
Even if it was only Tri, who was cute, but cute the way teddy
bears were cute. "Sure," she said, standing up and taking it.

She put her hands on Tri's shoulders and he put his
hands on her waist and they began to move to the waltz's box
step. Tri fumbled and stepped on her left foot, crushing her
toes. "Ow!" she yelped.

"Oops, sorry." Tri blushed. "Are you okay?" His dark cowlick fell into his bright blue eyes, and Ashley suddenly felt a flutter in her stomach. He was really very cute, she thought. How come she'd never noticed before?

They glided across the room and Ashley tingled, feeling the jealous, watchful eyes of all the girls focused hungrily on the two of them.

Then the classical music screeched to a halt. Ashley and Tri looked up at the stage, where DJ Tommy, out of breath and still wearing his St. Aloysius uniform, was now installed at the turntables and removing Miss Charm's Chopin record. Tommy shook his head and placed a new one on. He held a pair of earphones up to his ear with one hand, and with the other put the needle on the record.

He leaned into the mic. "MISS GAMBLE'S IN THE HOWWWSSSS!" he whooped. The hard beats of the latest felon rap, "Drank Me to Death," reverberated around the Little Theater.

Screaming girls rushed to the middle of the dance floor, tired of waiting to be asked. Ashley smiled and cheered silently for her sisters.

Who needs boys?

The dance had officially begun.

32

YOU GET WHAT YOU WISH FOR?

T RYING NOT TO FEEL TOO STUNG THAT TRI had asked Ashley to dance instead of her, A. A. crept along the side of the wall, avoiding the bodies crashing into one another on the dance floor. Boys were slamming into girls, girls were bouncing off one another. It was total bedlam, and not at all like the genteel mixer that the school had in mind. It was more like a flurry. Everyone blended. She was set to meet laxjock at Huntington Park in a few minutes.

It was weird to think that after months of texting, they would finally be able to meet. What if he wasn't as cute as she imagined? Or worse, what if he didn't think she was cute? Or what if he was perfectly nice, but not at all hot like his e-mails and text messages implied? She quickly wrapped a red Hermès scarf around her head while she dodged the flailing bodies of her classmates. She'd come up with the scarf as a way for him to recognize her. She told him she'd be wearing a printed red scarf, and laxjock had said he'd be wearing a black baseball cap.

She finally made it outside the auditorium and slipped out the school's back door and through the back alley that took her to upper Broadway. The park wasn't too far away, but she wanted to get there early to scope out the scene. She told herself that whoever laxjock turned out to be, she would stick it out and meet him. She wouldn't pull a disappearing act, even if he turned out to be a fat, homeschooled loser. *Please, don't turn out to be a fat, homeschooled loser*, she prayed.

Huntington Park was one of San Francisco's beautiful public squares, modeled after similar ones in Paris. When laxjock had suggested meeting there, A. A. had readily agreed. She'd always been fond of the Fountain of the Tortoises, a copy of the famous Roman fountain, which depicted water nymphs and cherubs prancing in the water, and had told him so. He said it was one of his favorite spots in San Francisco as well.

The park hummed with afternoon activities. There were dog walkers holding leashes to packs of dogs, a group of little kids from a nearby day care center at the children's playground, and several elderly couples sitting on the opposite benches taking in the fresh air.

She fiddled with her scarf and pulled it tightly around her

head. She had decided against her customary pigtails, fearing they would make her look too young. As the minutes ticked by, she thought of texting him again but forced herself not to. He would show up, she told herself. A. A. watched the water trickle down from a nymph's hands into the calm blue pool. She walked over and threw a quarter into the water, an investment in a wish. She was ready to meet the guy who'd made her heart beat ever since sending her that first romantic e-mail.

DO I KNOW U? she'd texted just a few days ago.

MAY-B, he'd replied. I'M CLOSER THAN U THINK.

The setting sun blinded her eyes, and she blinked. When the sunspots faded away, she could see clearly. There was a boy walking toward her.

Her heart thudded so hard in her chest she was sure the punk-rock couple making out in the bushes across the way could hear it.

The boy walking toward her was Dex Bond.

And he was wearing a black baseball cap.

33

REVENGE OF THE NERD

BACK AT MISS GAMBLE'S, LAUREN PAGE stood in front of the entrance to the Little Theater. She could hear the music throb from inside, so loudly that it shook the auditorium doors. It sounded like they were really tearing it up at five o'clock in the afternoon. Nobody could accuse private-school girls of not knowing how to par-tay.

She knew the Ashleys probably thought she had fled the city for good, or transferred over to Helena Academy, or spent the last four days in bed with the covers over her head. But none of that had happened.

Due to a happy coincidence, the day after the sleepover, her dad had been called away for a technology conference in Washington, and the whole family was invited to have dinner at the White House the day after that. Her mom decided to pull her out of school so she could join the dinner with the president's family, and afterward they had been stuck in the capital because freakishly bad weather had grounded all flights, including private jets.

They had returned to the city just that morning, and while part of her felt like disappearing into a dark hole and never coming out, the other part—the part that had been motivated enough to pursue a life-changing makeover and invite the Ashleys for a shopping spree on Robertson Boulevard—had come up with an alternative solution.

Sure, she could return to school and suffer through another round of the Ashleys' teasing and indifference. She could go back to eating her lunches alone in the computer room and keeping her head down in the hallways. She could go back to a thousand little indignities that made every day unpleasant.

Or she could do something about it.

She heard his footsteps behind her. This was just so perfect she couldn't help pinching herself. She turned around and smiled at her date.

Billy Reddy.

She was actually going to show up at the mixer with the great Billy Reddy at her side.

So she'd had to promise she was going to get the whole upper form to watch the next Gregory Hall lacrosse game. But how hard could that be? Dex had told her the team had made the play-offs, but it was a pity that Reed Prep, their opponent, had a huge fan section since it was a coed school, while Gregory Hall was all boys.

"Cheerleaders," Dex had said. "We need cheerleaders."

As if the Ashleys would turn down a chance to show off their dance-team moves.

She pushed open the door, feeling her skin tingle with anticipation. It was dark inside the Little Theater, and she couldn't see very well with all the flashing strobe lights, but she could make out the forms of Ashley Spencer and Ashley Li onstage, dancing in a circle with several Gregory Hall boys.

As usual, the Ashleys had commandeered the best location, the place where everyone could see them and they could look down over everyone. They always maneuvered it so that they were on top of everything.

Well, not this time.

34

SOMEDAY YOUR PRINCE
WILL COME?

DEX WALKED BRISKLY TOWARD THE
fountain. He was wearing a black baseball cap
and carrying a bouquet of roses. A. A. felt so
elated she couldn't even speak for a moment. *It's him. I knew it.*
He looked even more handsome than she remembered.

She couldn't stand it anymore. "Dex!" she called, waving.

He broke stride and looked around. Then he spotted
her, and a big, goofy grin came over his face. "Hey, Ashley
Alioto, right?" he asked, squinting at her.

"Dexter Bond," she said coyly.

He sat on the bench next to her and placed the bouquet
of flowers between them.

A. A. tugged on the Hermès scarf. It was a present from
the fashion house to her mother for starring in one of their

ad campaigns a long time ago. She'd figured it would look nice with her dark hair. "I'm wearing *red*," she said, thinking it was an odd way to start a conversation with laxjock—Dex—but she felt suddenly shy.

Online, she could tell laxjock anything. But now that he was actually sitting next to her, it was like she'd hit the mute button. But when he didn't respond, she tried again. "And you've got a black baseball cap on."

"Yeah. Giants game later today," he said, craning his neck to watch the kids down by the playground.

A. A. felt a chill in the air, even though there was no breeze. This was so not the way she'd pictured it happening. He hadn't even handed her the flowers yet. She let out a short, sharp laugh. Then she noticed that there were other guys in the park, and most of them were wearing black Giants baseball caps. The city must be filled with guys wearing them.

"You have no idea what I'm talking about, do you?" she asked.

"Talking about what?" Dex said. He smiled at her, but his eyes were focused on the playground.

The small seed of doubt began to sprout, take root, and flourish. "And those aren't for me either?" she asked, pointing at the flowers.

To his credit, Dex, ever the gentleman, didn't respond in the negative right away. "Er . . ."

The hope in A. A.'s heart began to wither. "No, it's okay. I don't even know why I asked." Only then did she notice that there was a reason Dex kept looking over to the children's playground. The kindergarten teacher was very pretty. A. A. looked over at Dex and knew the truth.

"How long have you been dating her?" she asked.

Dex clasped his hands behind his back. "That obvious, huh?" He smiled sheepishly. "She's twenty-five, a little old for me. So I like to keep it on the down low." He picked up the flowers on the bench. "Do you think she'll like them?"

A. A. nodded. "She'll love them."

"Nice seeing you, Alioto. Hey, shouldn't you be at some dance?" he said.

"I'm meeting someone," she explained.

"Ah." Dex nodded and took his leave. She watched him approach the kindergarten teacher shyly. The girl looked delighted at the sight of the flowers.

Then A. A. looked at her phone. No texts. No messages. It was an hour after they said they'd meet.

Whoever laxjock was, he wasn't coming.

35

ASHLEY SPENCER DOESN'T
SETTLE FOR SLOPPY SECONDS

OTHING COULD EVER TAKE ASHLEY Spencer off guard, and if she was surprised to see Lauren Page arrive at the dance on the arm of Billy Reddy, she didn't show it. She watched the two of them make their way over to where she was standing.

"You're alive," she said flatly to Lauren.

"As far as I know, you can't die of embarrassment," Lauren replied. "Ashley, have you met . . ."

"I'm Billy Reddy," said Billy, extending his hand over the seafood platters in front of them at the buffet station.

"Hi." Ashley smiled, shaking it. He was absolutely gorgeous. The tousled hair, the toothpaste-commercial smile. But somehow Billy didn't look as cute up close as he did from afar. It was like the time her parents took her to an American

Idol concert, and they'd been able to go backstage and she'd met the stud she'd been crushing on for so long her fingers would bleed from voting for him a hundred times every week on her cell phone. It was kind of anticlimactic to realize that he was just some normal guy, who looked shorter than he was on TV and had a little body odor from performing.

Billy Reddy didn't smell, but now that he was standing right in front of her with his hand out, he didn't seem to be the Cutest Boy in the World, either. He was just some good-looking guy. And there were tons of good-looking guys in the city. Besides, what high school sophomore would be caught at a dance with seventh graders? Wasn't that a bit creepy-geeky? And he was with Lauren. As her date. Gag.

"I'm Lili," Lili said, coming between them.

Billy and Lili began to talk, and Ashley moved down the buffet line. She had assumed correctly, there was nothing she could eat on the menu. She was glad she'd bullied Lili into ordering the special cupcakes. At least she would be able to eat those. She felt a nudge on her arm and turned around to see Lauren standing next to her.

"So you've finally met Billy," Lauren said.

"Yeah." Ashley shrugged.

Lauren looked physically deflated. "Listen—I'm really sorry about what happened the other day. I know I overreacted. I didn't mean what I said."

"That's fine," said Ashley. "But it doesn't change any-thing."

"Why not?" Lauren cried, her voice inching up another octave. The girl really needed to chill out.

"It just doesn't. Oh, there's Tri," Ashley said, as Tri walked up carrying a plate of mini cupcakes. Just what she was looking for.

"Want one?" he asked. He was so thoughtful. The perfect gentleman.

"Sure," she said, picking up one of the delicious-looking treats and taking a bite.

Lauren was still standing next to her, looking lost and uncertain.

"Shoo," Ashley told her. "Leave me and my friends alone, zero."

"What was that?" Tri asked, looking curiously from Ashley to Lauren.

"Nothing," Ashley dismissed. She took another bite of the cupcake. "I was just saying . . ." Then she realized that she couldn't breathe. And that her mouth was on fire. There was something horribly, horribly wrong. But before she could think of what it was, she blacked out.

36

BUTTERCREAM CUPCAKE, OR
AGENT OF DEATH?

SOMEONE WAS SCREAMING. LILI TORE herself away from Billy's side and ran over to where Lauren was standing over Ashley's prone body. Ashley was just lying there, clutching a cupcake in one hand.

"What did you do to her?" Lili accused.

"I didn't do anything!" cried Lauren. "She just fell!"

"Nobody just falls!" Lili screamed. "Ashley? Ashley? Can you hear me?" She knelt down by Ashley's body. It was still warm. She shook her. Hard.

"What the hell happened?" Lili demanded.

"Nothing, she was just standing there, and then she hit the ground." said Lauren.

"Well, something must have happened!"

Lili looked at Lauren. "What are you doing back at school, anyway? I thought you were dead."

"I'm not dead," Lauren retorted. "Is that what you guys told everyone about me? I was wondering why everyone was looking at me funny."

Lili didn't respond. She picked up Ashley's hand and tried to feel a pulse, but she was so panicked she couldn't figure out if she could feel anything. A rising tide of emotion swept over her. Ashley Spencer was dead. So why did she feel . . . happy?

"What's happened?"

A voice brought her back to her senses. Lili turned around. A. A. stood there, her cheeks flushed. She had on a red scarf that she hadn't been wearing earlier.

"Thank God you're here," said Lili, pushing away all thoughts of how she would be the most popular girl in the class now that Ashley had met her demise. "It's Ashley!"

"Hey—should we call 911 or something?" said Billy Reddy, walking over. A few more people began to surround them, to see what the commotion was all about.

"What's wrong with her?" A. A. asked, dropping down on Ashley's other side.

"I told you, we were just talking and then she fell. No, wait." Lauren shook her head. "She took a bite of the cupcake and then she fell. What was in those cupcakes, Lili?"

"Nothing. They're just cupcakes. Plain vanilla cupcakes."

"When she took a bite, she had some sort of spasm before she passed out. It could be an allergic reaction. Is she allergic to anything?" asked Lauren.

"No. Not as far as I know," Lili said, shaking her head. What was Ashley allergic to? Nerds? Zits? Bad fashion?

"Peanuts! She's allergic to peanuts," A. A. said suddenly. "She told me last month after the tea when I asked her why she wouldn't eat any of the scones when they were so yummy. And she asked the waiter at the Ivy if there were any nuts in her salad. She always does that. Remember how at the sleepover she admitted she didn't know what peanut butter tasted like?"

"But there aren't any peanuts in the cupcakes," Lili said. "I told you, they're just plain vanilla!"

"But peanuts could be anywhere. In the batter. In the frosting. Lots of things are made with nuts. Ashley said almost anything can have trace amount of nuts, which is why she only eats food prepared by their chef," said A. A.

"Omigod!" Lili wailed. So that's why Ashley wanted the cupcakes made from a special recipe. Except she had told the bakery to go ahead and make their usual batch.

"I've killed my best friend!" Lili screamed. *This is the worst and best day of my life.*

37

DING-DONG, THE WITCH
IS DEAD?

'VE KILLED ASHLEY SPENCER, LAUREN thought. *This is the best and worst day of my life.* She was the one who had convinced Lili to forget about the special recipe and just order the regular cupcakes. *What she doesn't know won't hurt her.* She'd just assumed Ashley was being precious and diva-like. She didn't know Ashley was allergic. Did they have jail sentences for twelve-year-olds? But it was an accident!

"Somebody do something!" A. A. screamed.

Then Lauren remembered something she'd read in *Teen Vogue* during her makeover madness, when she was boning up on how to be an Ashley. There'd been an article on a girl with a peanut allergy, and the article had talked about what to do in case of an emergency. Lauren knelt down and lifted the hem on Ashley's skirt, stopping to admire the dress. It was really cute. Kate Moss Topshop? It had to be.

"Stop that! What are you doing?" Lili demanded.

"Saving her life," said Lauren. "She has to have it somewhere on her body. That's the only way. Yes. Here it is." Lauren pushed the skirt aside and showed them.

Ashley was wearing some kind of garter on her thigh, and tucked into the garter was a slim silver pen. But Lauren knew that instead of a ballpoint it held a needle. The article said that all people who suffered from a nut allergy had to carry it on their person. The girl in the article carried it on her thigh, and knowing how much of a slave Ashley was to *Teen Vogue*, it was no surprise that she did the same thing.

"It's an antidote. I have to give it to her now, if she's going to make it," Lauren said, taking the needle—an EpiPen, the article had called it.

"Do it!" yelled A. A.

"One, two, three," Lauren said. Then she poked Ashley in the arm with the needle.

Lauren thought Ashley would immediately sit up and spring back to life. But instead, nothing happened. Ashley still looked dead. Her eyes were closed. Her face was blue. She wasn't breathing.

It was too late.

Lauren sighed. She was definitely going to jail. She would

never get into Exeter now. She imagined her future. On the one hand, it would be a lot better now that Ashley Spencer wasn't around to tell all the kids in class that she was a loser. But on the other hand, she would be in jail. Did they have Advanced Placement classes in Juvenile Hall? Sure, she had wanted Ashley taken down. Destroyed. But not in the literal sense. She wasn't a psycho.

Then Ashley blinked and opened her eyes. She looked around. She saw the EpiPen in Lauren's hand, the surrounding crowd of onlookers, and her skirt bunched around her waist.

"Omigod!" Ashley gasped. "Did all these boys see my underwear?"

38

THE DANGER OF LOOKING
FOR LOVE IN ALL THE
WRONG PLACES

ASHLEY WAS ALIVE. THANK GOD FOR Lauren's quick thinking. She'd saved her life. A. A. gave a huge sigh of relief. Knowing that her best friend would live took the sting out of being stood up by laxjock. So it wasn't Dex after all. But who could it be? She had no idea.

Ashley was still on the ground, complaining about how her privacy had been invaded, and Lili and Lauren were fighting to get her a glass of water. Billy Reddy was standing around, looking completely flabbergasted by the turn of events. She bet none of the high school parties he'd ever been to were as action-packed as this.

Then she noticed Tri standing to the side, frozen, a plate of cupcakes in his hand.

"Hey," she said. "You okay? You look weird."

"I almost killed her," Tri whispered. "I gave her that cupcake."

"Hey, don't worry about it. You didn't know she was allergic."

"I almost killed her," he repeated.

A. A. shook her head. It wasn't like Tri to be so dramatic. Then she noticed something. A black baseball cap folded into the pocket of his blazer. A black San Francisco Giants baseball cap. Tri's favorite team. His favorite baseball cap. He always wore that cap. She remembered something else, too—at the dance, he'd asked her if she was getting ready to go to the fountain. How did he know about meeting laxjock at the fountain? She'd never told him.

She looked at Tri. He was her best friend. The only person she could tell everything to. The only person who would know what to say to all her problems. He'd given her a perfect score on the rank call.

Tri Fitzpatrick was laxjock.

But he hadn't shown up to meet her at the park. Because she'd told him she'd suspected the love of her life was Dex Bond. Some random guy who didn't even know her at all. She felt her heart clench. Tri . . .

"Tri," she gulped.

But Tri wasn't listening. He was completely ignoring her.

He put down the plate of cupcakes and ran over to Ashley's side. There was a strange new light in his eyes. As if he were seeing Ashley Spencer for the first time.

Then he was helping Ashley to her feet, and he was looking at her in the same way A. A. now realized he'd been looking at A. A. herself for months.

With total, complete adoration.

EPILOGUES

Dear Diary,

We're supposed to keep a diary for English class now. To write about what's happening in our life so we can understand it better. Or something like that. Anyway, here goes.

So the beast still lives. Yes, Ashley Spencer survived to mock for another day. She's fully recovered from her adverse reaction to eating a trace amount of nuts in the vanilla cupcake at the dance. Except for a tiny rash that went away all too quickly.

I didn't get to join the Ashleys and I didn't get to destroy them either. But Nut Day, as I'm calling the dance, did score a small victory for those of us on the bottom of the seventh-grade social pyramid.

Since Ashley Spencer had to come clean about her nut allergy, poor Cass Franklin doesn't have to sit in a quarantined place in the refectory anymore. Thanks to Ashley, the whole refectory is a quarantine. Her parents threatened to sue the school because of the incident, and now

all they serve in the ref is spelt bread and yogurt. Yum.
Not.

Plus, you'd think that having a spasm in public would
mean the end of Ashley's ironclad reign. But no. Instead,
because of the EpiPen in her garter, garters are now the
latest accessory at Miss Gamble's. The latest thing is to
wear them like Ashley's, underneath the uniform skirt, so
when you sit down they peek out.

This just proves that the entire seventh grade is just nuts.
So then wouldn't Ashley be allergic to everyone?

But still. Ashley has to start being nice to me, right? I
saved her life. Doesn't that count for something?

I hope so.

Anxiously,

Lauren Page

JOURNAL.DOC

This is so silly, because I've been keeping a diary since I was in first grade. My mom says it's the only way to organize your thoughts. And you know that's what I am. Organized.

I still feel really guilty for almost having killed my best friend. Especially for feeling happy about it. But later, when I thought about it, I realized my happiness was only hiding what I really felt. And what I really felt was hurt. Deeply, deeply hurt. I totally would never have ordered the regular cupcakes if Ashley had told me she was allergic! She told A. A., but not me. So part of it was her fault, right? How could she keep a secret that big from me?

I confronted her with it, and she didn't deny it. She said she was sorry and that she had kept other secrets from me too. So then I had to be honest with her, too, and told her I thought her anime thermos was ugly. A. A. told us to shut up already.

We had a few tears. But then we had hugs. And then the three of us went to Tiffany and bought these gold necklaces to wear, each with a charm that was one-third of a heart. Ashley got the biggest piece, of course.

Still, I'm so glad Ashley isn't dead. Because who else is going to lend me her Kate Moss for Topshop dress?

Yours in relief,

Lili

MEMO: FILE: DIARY: ALIOTO, ASHLEY

2DAY I WISHED 2 OF MY BFFS WERE DEAD. I
JUST CAN'T B-LIEVE THE 2 OF THEM ARE
2GETHER. OMG. IT'S NOT LIKE I CARE U
KNOW? REALLY, IT'S GR8.
IF THEY'RE HAPPY 2GETHER THEN I'M HAPPY
4 THEM, RIGHT?
SO WHY AM I NOT HAPPY?
:(

Hello? Is this on? Yeah. We're supposed to keep a diary for English, but I thought I'd speak into this iPod recorder instead and have my maid transcribe my thoughts. Who has time to type? Hello.

Okay, so Lauren Page saved my life. Bee. Eff. Dee. It was the least she could do after almost killing me! She owed it to me. Okay, so maybe I will stop ragging on her a little bit, stop telling people that she *planned* to kill me.

Life is different on the other side of the tunnel. Not that I saw a white light or anything. I just kind of zoned out there a little bit. But now that I think about it, I'm really lucky to have survived. I mean, I could have died. At a dance! How embarrassing.

Like I said, things have changed. Lili is a lot nicer to me, but A. A. is kind of withdrawn. I don't know what she's got a bug in her butt about. I mean, it's not like she ever said she liked him. She always said they were just friends.

I mean, Tri may be short, but he is super-cute. And he's only going to get taller. I can wait. I know A. A. thinks he was laxjock, but he's never owned up to it. And she had her chance with him.

So as far as I can tell, *finders keepers*.

ACKNOWLEDGMENTS

As always, thanks very much to my wonderful peeps at Simon & Schuster. I heart you all, especially my sassy, smart, and chic editor, Emily "Ashley" Meehan, and her partner in crime, Courtney "Ashley" Bongiolatti.

Many thanks to all my family and friends for their love and support. Thanks especially to the team: Christina Green, Arisa Chen, and Jennie Kim. Thanks to Richard Abate and his team at Endeavor, and Jossie Freedman and Katie Lee and their team at ICM.

Thanks to my husband, Mike Johnston, for being endlessly patient while listening to my nonstop recollections of junior high and sharing some of his own.

And last but totally not least, hugs, kisses, and a huge shout-out to all my super-cute readers whose comments, e-mails, IMs, and letters always brighten my day.

ABOUT THE AUTHOR

Melissa de la Cruz is the author of many books for teens, including the bestselling series The Au Pairs, Blue Bloods, and Angels on Sunset Boulevard. Her books for adults include the anthology *Girls Who Like Boys Who Like Boys* and the tongue-in-chic handbook *The Fashionista Files: Adventures in Four-inch Heels and Faux Pas*. Melissa has written for many publications, including *Teen Vogue*, *Seventeen*, and *CosmoGIRL!*, and sometimes appears on television as an expert on style, trends, and fame.

A graduate of Columbia University, she was salutatorian of her class at the Convent of the Sacred Heart High School in San Francisco. In seventh grade she was the only girl asked by the Billy Reddy of her day to dance at the first boy-girl party. Alas, he was not her type (too pretty!). She is happily married to a handsome architect, and they live in the Hollywood Hills with their adorable baby daughter. She still believes that if you eat Pop Rocks and Coke, you could die.

Check out her website at www.melissa-delacruz.com and e-mail her at melissa@melissa-delacruz.com. She always responds to her readers!

Want to find out what
happens next to

th**e**ashleys?

Here's a sneak peek at
book 2 in The Ashleys series,
Jealous?

A MODEL HOMECOMING

"HONEY, I'VE MISSED YOU SO MUCH!"

"I missed you too, Mom." Ashley Alioto—otherwise known as A. A., one of the tween triumvirate of Ashleys who were the acknowledged social elite of Miss Gamble's School for Girls—smiled up at her mother.

Jeanine Alioto was as beautiful as ever, tall and willowy, her long dark hair perfectly razor cut and blow-dried, her eyebrows immaculately threaded, her lips injected with just enough Venezuelan bee serum to make her mouth a seductive pout. Sometimes girls at school—non-Ashleys, of course—asked her if it was a drag having a former supermodel for a mother, as though getting great genes (not to mention an endless supply of great jeans) was a bad thing.

The only kind-of-bad part was when her mother disappeared for weeks at a time because some rich guy wanted her to sail around the Caribbean or hang out at the Cannes

Film Festival with him. A. A. was left at home in their penthouse apartment in the Fairmont Hotel with her half brother, Ned. They got along just fine without Jeanine—duh, room service!—but it was always better when her mother was home, not least because she always brought back a ton of cool gifts.

"And these are for you, Lili," said her mother, pulling a chic pair of black shoes from one of her overflowing Goyard suitcases and tossing them into the eager hands of Ashley Li, known as Lili since the fourth grade, when Ashley Spencer, in her typically imperious way, decided that one Ashley was enough.

The shoes meant for Lili had three-inch curvy heels and their ankle straps fastened with a tiny ribbon. Receiving designer swag was just another one of the many perks of being an Ashley, but Lili, perched on the edge of the buttercolored chaise lounge, peered at them with a puzzled smile on her face.

"Thanks so much, Jeanine," she said in her peppiest voice, but A. A. knew what she was thinking. Lili was a total brand queen, and if she didn't recognize the name imprinted in the soft calfskin soles of the shoes, then they might as well be a pair of sweaty Crocs. "Are these an Argentinian . . . er, specialty?"

"Sweetie, they're tango shoes!" Jeanine scrambled to her feet. In her skin-tight Ksubi jeans tucked into calf-high Fiorentini and Baker boots she was more than six feet tall, towering over the petite Lili and even over A. A., who'd inherited her mother's long, lean physique but was currently sprawled out on the white sheepskin rug. "I got them for A. A. and then remembered she'd rather throw herself around on a soccer field than do anything ladylike, and I know you're the same size. I spent a few days in Buenos Aires at the tango festival, and these are from *the* tango shoe store. Everything's handmade and super expensive."

"I'd love to learn the tango," sighed Lili, flicking her glossy jet-black hair, a dreamy expression floating over her pretty, heart-shaped face. A. A. let out a snort of laughter: All Lili needed was yet another extracurricular activity! When she wasn't taking violin or tennis lessons, she was brushing up on her French and Mandarin language skills, or learning how to take expert photographs, or helping a Stanford professor with his genetics research. If A. A. had Lili's over-scheduled life, she'd go crazy.

"I thought you were going to Brazil." A. A. picked at the intricately woven blue hammock her mother had pulled from suitcase number one twenty minutes ago. There was an outdoor terrace off the suite where it would hang perfectly.

"Rio in the off-season just isn't me," Jeanine sighed, mussing her luxuriant dark locks. "The Copa is no fun in the rain, and I was sick of looking at all those undernourished girls from Ipanema hanging around and hoping to get discovered by Victoria's Secret."

A. A. rolled onto her stomach and rested her head in her hands. She loved it when her mother started dishing on the modeling world. Jeanine always called herself the "Last of the Supermodels," talking about the good old days when the top models were known by their first names alone, everyone had major attitude and the breasts to go with it, and affairs with celebrities were de rigueur—her second husband, Ned's father, was a British rock star. These days, she said, the girls were barely old enough to date, and all the magazine covers were hogged by skanky Hollywood starlets.

"And anyway," Jeanine continued, back on her knees and rifling through her suitcase again, "Gil was thinking of buying some gaucho ranch in Argentina, so we flew down there."

Gil was Richard Gilbert, the software tycoon Jeanine had been dating on and off for the past six months. A. A. thought he was okay, if a little too earnest and big-skies-of-Montana for her liking: He was always going on about the heartland and about getting back to nature, which seemed pretty ironic for a guy who'd made his fortune selling technology. She and Ned had already decided they didn't want him as a stepfather, but it was too soon to worry—Jeanine's relationships had a habit of self-combusting before too many commitments were made.

"Did you and Mr. Gilbert learn to dance the tango while you were there?" Lili had already slipped off her Tory Burch flats and was carefully tying the delicate ribbons of the tango shoes around her slim ankles.

"I don't know what *Mr. Gilbert* was doing," said Jeanine, her voice dripping with sarcasm. "After three days of galloping around in the mud wearing a poncho, I'd had enough. And let's just say horses weren't the only thing he was checking out in Argentina."

She tugged a vibrant purple-patterned silk scarf out of her bag and draped it over A. A.'s shoulders, and then rummaged for another one, this time a swirling, kaleidoscopic mix of greens and pinks.

"For you," said Jeanine, wafting it at Lili. "These are just Pucci—I picked them up at the airport when my flight back was delayed. I grabbed a blue one for Ashley Spencer too, because I know how you three *have* to have the same things."

"So you and Gil have broken up?" A. A. tried not to sound too pleased. She sat up to adjust her trademark pigtails and loop the scarf around her neck.

"Let's just say I need someone who's man enough to tango with me and me alone," Jeanine said, rocking back on her heels and shooting them her famous, wicked, *Cosmo*-cover smile. "And you know what I always tell you, girls."

"Leave them while you're still looking good!" chorused A. A. and Lili, laughing. For the millionth time in her life—all twelve years of it—A. A. felt relieved and happy that her mother was so much fun, more of a friend than a mom. It was so easy to talk to her. Everything was better when Jeanine was home—even if she did insist on redecorating their luxurious penthouse suite way too often. As long as she didn't let her snooty decorator banish A. A. and Ned's vast video-game collection or downsize the flat-screen TV in the loft-size living room, they wouldn't complain.

"So what's been going on at Hogwarts?" her mother asked, pulling the Pucci scarf away from A. A. and tying it in an effortlessly chic headband around her own hair.

"Social Club had its first coed mixer with the Gregory Hall boys," Lili told her, "which I pretty much organized—"

"Pretty much nearly murdering Ashley at the same time," interrupted A. A., and then they both scrambled to fill Jeanine in on the crazy events of just a week ago. The vanilla cupcakes Lili'd ordered had triggered Ashley Spencer's serious nut allergy, and she'd ended up unconscious on the dance floor.

No one had known about Ashley's allergy, except A. A., who'd only remembered Ashley's secret when Ashley-wannabe and terminal-dork Lauren Page had asked if Ashley happened to be allergic to anything. If it hadn't been for quick thinking on Lauren's part, Lili would be facing a future in juvenile hall rather than Groton, her prep school of choice.

"Sounds like you all owe this girl Lauren," said Jeanine. Outside a light rain pattered against the tiles of the terrace, and she reached for the remote control, instantly conjuring up a flickering fire in the white granite fireplace.

A. A. and Lili exchanged glances: That climber Lauren was still in social Siberia—that is, unless Ashley decided otherwise. And all Ashley had gone on about since the dance was Tri Fitzpatrick. Tri, the boy who A. A. had known forever, her video-game buddy. The boy who was the cutest (and shortest) seventh grader at Gregory Hall. The boy who was supposed to be mad keen on *her*, not Ashley. She couldn't bear to even think about it.

"Lauren's old news. Everyone's talking about something else now," she told her mother. "At the beginning of this week, the weirdest thing happened."

"There's a website," Lili chimed in, her voice as animated as her face. "Nobody knows who's behind it!"

"But it's someone at our school—it has to be." A. A. pulled off her cashmere socks and wriggled her bare toes.

"Everyone's addicted," Lili added breathlessly. "You have to check it every day."

"They say we're the ones who did it, but it's got nothing to do with us," A. A. insisted.

"What are you girls talking about?" Jeanine asked, emptying her giant makeup bag onto the polished wood floor and grabbing a Chanel nail polish bottle before it rolled away.

"The website," A. A. explained. "It's www.ashleyrank.com. That's why everyone thinks the Ashleys started it."

"All the seventh-grade girls are ranked according to how popular and powerful they are. It's addictive. You know," Lili said with a smirk, "like watching Shark Week. A feeding frenzy. Who gets to rule the ocean—or in this case, seventh grade." She reached into her beige Fendi Spy bag and retrieved her BlackBerry, frowning a little as she tapped on the miniature screen. "Here it is. Ashleyrank, one through thirty-six."

"Cass Franklin is number thirty-six," A. A. told her mother. She didn't have to check the site again because she'd already memorized the key details. "That's the girl I told you about, the one who should be living in a plastic bubble. She has to keep an oxygen tank in her bag in case of emergency. It's social death."

"More to the point," said Lili in her brisk Honor Board voice, "the Ashleys hold the top three spots. That's why everyone thinks we came up with this."

"And you're sure you didn't?" Jeanine sounded amused.

"I know *I* didn't," A. A. said.

"I certainly didn't." Lili was indignant, and A. A. knew why: Lili was the number three Ashley, behind A. A. and, at number one, the self-appointed Queen Bee of Miss Gamble's herself, Ashley Spencer.

The intercom chimed, and the front desk clerk announced another guest. A. A. told him to let her in: It was Ashley, arriving for her share of the South American fashion loot.

That girl must have ESP. Jeanine was about to open the next suitcase and start pulling out fabulous clothes for her daughter to try on. Anything A. A. didn't want, Lili and Ashley could grab, and it was always funny watching them fight over A. A.'s leftovers.

The private elevator that opened directly into the apartment dinged.

"Hey, Ash, right on time as usual," A. A. called, looking up with a grin that soon disappeared from her pretty face.

Because when the elevator doors opened, and Ashley—cool, blond, and stylishly dressed, as usual—strolled in, she wasn't alone. Holding her hand in the lamest and most embarrassing way, and gazing up at her with adoring puppy-dog eyes as though they were actually, yuckily, *in love*, was Tri Fitzpatrick.

THE ASHLEYS: JEALOUS?

By Melissa de la Cruz

Coming April 2008

WANT TO DRESS LIKE AN ASHLEY?

Go to **www.behindthepulse.com/ashleys**
and enter to win a shopping spree.

NO PURCHASE NECESSARY